Read

Ia

Village of a Million Spirits
"One of the best books of the year"
—*L.A. Times*

"...a new benchmark in Holocaust literature"
—*Publishers Weekly*

"...thoroughly convincing, ruthlessly absorbing...stands as a testament to the proposition that a well-chosen word is worth a thousand pictures"
—*Jerusalem Post*

"Incredibly powerful historical fiction"
—*Chicago Tribune*

"a shivery, heart-stunning piece of work"
—*Newsday*

"The impact of *Village of a Million Spirits* is so forceful that it negates the question such a fictionalization of the Holocaust raises: Why turn to art to dramatize an already intensely dramatic factual event? Eloquently, MacMillan shows that the truth we can absolutely, factually know...it is not the whole story...to understand completely, we must go beyond all this to the rest of the story, to tell the truth... the only way to get at that truth is to imagine it. And the only way to imagine it is through art."
—*New York Times Book Review*

The Red Wind
"*Red Wind* is a saga in the very best sense of the word"
—*The Honolulu Advertiser*

Squid Eye
"Here's a book that brings you eye to eye with life in Hawai'i—not the flowery, painted-over stuff but the real nitty-gritty"
—*The Honolulu Advertiser*

Other Books by

Ian MacMillan

Light and Power, University of Missouri Press, 1980

Blakely's Ark, Berkeley/Putnam, 1981

Proud Monster, North Point Press, 1987

Orbit of Darkness, Harcourt, Brace, Jovanovich, 1991

Exiles from Time, Anoai Press, 1998

The Red Wind, Mutual Publishing, 1998

Village of a Million Spirits: A Novel of the Treblinka Uprising,
Steerforth Press and Penguin Books, 2000

Squid Eye, Anoai Press, 1999

Ullambana, Anoai Press, 2002

The Seven Orchids, University of Hawai'i Press, 2006

The Braid, Mutual Publishing, 2005

Our People , BkMk Press, 2008

Stories in Collections

"The Red House," *Prize Stories: The O. Henry Awards*, 1997.
"from Proud Monster," *Best American Short Stories*, 1982.
"The Unknown Soldier Passes," *Pushcart Prize: Best of the Small Presses*, 1978-79.
"Sacrifice," *Best of TriQuarterly*, 1982.
"The Rock," *A Hawai'i Anthology*, 1997.
"Liar Liar," *The Quietest Singing* (anthology of writing from Hawai'i, UH Press), 2000.

the Bone Hook

A Novel

the Bone Hook

A Novel

Ian MacMillan

MUTUAL PUBLISHING

A version of this essay first appeared in Bamboo Ridge Issue 94 (Fall 2009)

Library of Congress Cataloging-in-Publication Data available upon request.
ISBN-10: 1-56647-876-6
ISBN-13: 978-1-56647-876-2

Design by Courtney Young

First Printing, October 2009

Mutual Publishing, LLC
1215 Center Street, Suite 210
Honolulu, Hawai'i 96816
Ph: 808-732-1709 / Fax: 808-734-4094
email: info@mutualpublishing.com
www.mutualpublishing.com

Printed in Taiwan

For Susan, Julia, Laura, Rick and Emma

Foreword

The Bone Hook, Ian MacMillan's third novel with Mutual Publishing, is published posthumously. Ian passed away—too soon—in 2008. He was an invaluable contributor to literature in Hawai'i, and the words that follow remember him for this.

In the Mail
An Homage to Fiction Writer Ian MacMillan
by Julie Lynn Mitchell

Fiction writer Ian MacMillan was always a renegade when it came to writing. Stubbornly independent, mentorless, and just plain lucky, he stuck to his stylistic guns despite feedback from others–and encouraged new writers to do the same. His motto: "I am in the mail, therefore I am."

"If you have something you like, what's the point of leaving it in a drawer? The more you have in the mail the better your chances are. It's as simple as that," stated MacMillan who, when he died of cancer on December 18, 2008, had been 'in the mail' for over four decades.

A prolific writer, MacMillan authored eight novels and five short story collections. His short fiction appeared in over 100 literary and commercial magazines, and was reprinted in Pushcart Prize, Best American Short Stories, and O. Henry Award volumes as well as other anthologies. His books have been published by large and small presses, both with and without the help of agents.

MacMillan's most recent novels are *The Bone Hook* (Mutual Publishing, 2009), *The Seven Orchids* (Bamboo Ridge Press, 2006) and *The Braid* (Mutual Publishing, 2005). All three are set and published in Hawai'i, where he lived and taught for 42 years. Occasionally MacMillan flew from his home on O'ahu to teach and give readings on the Big Island for the non-profit Volcano Art Center.

MacMillan and I met on a rainy Sunday morning in a Volcano Village bed and breakfast, where he and his wife Susan—always his first reader/editor, and his photographer—spent the night. Skin tan and slightly weathered, MacMillan had an athlete's lean physique. Short silver-gray hair, beard, and mustache framed his sharp blue eyes, triangular nose, and broad forehead. He donned typical tropical attire: T-shirt, shorts, flip-flops.

He filled his coffee mug three times while we talked and, after bouts of fidgeting, took smoke breaks out on the lanai. During our meeting, MacMillan sat with his left elbow propped on the back of a chair—his left hand gesturing from its spot up high, his right hand gesticulating in front of his torso as he spoke. He often ended his sentences with a rhetorical "right?" or "see?"

"My father was an alcoholic," said MacMillan, born March 23, 1941 in Teaneck, New Jersey. Since his father had difficulty keeping jobs, their family lived in a number of suburban New Jersey towns until MacMillan hit 14, when his father read The Farm by Louis Bromfield and got hooked on the notion of country life.

They moved into an old farmhouse in a remote section of upstate New York, which MacMillan described as "depressed dairy country." His mother passed away shortly thereafter, and his father found work in Syracuse, leaving MacMillan and his two brothers to tend the place on their own. The three boys cut logs and pulped wood to try to make ends meet, but the family lost the farm just after MacMillan turned 16. His older brother joined the military, while he and the youngest became wards of the state and joined a nearby foster family until high school graduation. Sick with cancer, his father died in 1960.

MacMillan attended what he affectionately called a "cow college" because of its rural location. The State University of New York at Oneonota was the state normal school, training future public schoolteachers. "Most of the people there were 'normal,'" joked MacMillan, "but fortunately there were about 10 or 12 freaks at my school. You know, people who were into art and drama and stuff like that. So I moved over to hanging out with those people." And became, he said, a "surly, quiet freak" himself.

MacMillan's first passion was art but in his junior year he started writing fiction. "I never took a creative writing class. It's just that the freaks were writing, so I wrote. There was a small literary magazine that they ran. And I suppose I have to admit that some of the most exotic girls hung out at the literary magazine, one of whom is standing right over there," he said while pointing to Susan, with whom he was married 45 years.

During his senior year, MacMillan wrote a short story that his cohorts suggested he send out, and on a whim he submitted the piece to *The Carolina Quarterly*. "But, the magazine took it, see?" he marveled, "So, that changed everything. That's why I'm here. Because I got the one story published."

Donald Petersen, a poet teaching at SUNY, encouraged him to apply to the University of Iowa Writers' Workshop, which he didn't know existed. MacMillan—a poor-to-middling student who'd never taken standardized tests like the SAT—had no idea how to apply to a graduate program. Peterson advised him and, an Iowa alumnus himself, wrote MacMillan a letter of recommendation. On the strength of his application and single published piece, MacMillan got invited to the most prestigious Master of Fine Arts writing program in the country.

Entering in 1963, his fellow students included Raymond Carver, Andre Dubus, and Joy Williams; his teachers, R. V. Cassill and Kurt Vonnegut, Jr. MacMillan recalled being called into Cassill's office about one of his stories: "He wrote this sentence out and said, 'Here's how you begin this story.' But I couldn't make myself do it. So I sent the story out and it was accepted, almost immediately. And I thought, 'Oh my god, I can't ever let him see it'...laughs.... Because I left the first page just as I had written it."

MacMillan realized then that, where his words were at stake, he could never do what anybody said he ought to. "I'm not sure that I ever really had what people called a mentor. In fact I always felt a little funny because I remember I was always more sort of mulishly self-directed."

In his final year, an acquaintance encouraged MacMillan to sit for a job interview with a representative from the University of Hawai'i at Manoa. And on the first (and only) interview of his life—without knowing a thing about Hawai'i or having any teaching experience—he got hired as a writing instructor. When MacMillan landed on the island of O'ahu in 1966, his first assignment was a senior level workshop. "A third of the people in class were older than I was," stated MacMillan, who at 25 had less than a handful of published stories to his name.

MacMillan eventually became a tenured professor of English and taught creative writing to countless students during his four-plus decades at the university. He was the fiction editor for *MANOA: A Pacific Journal of International Writing* and the recipient of the 1992 Hawai'i Award for Literature, the state's highest literary honor, as well as the 2007 Cades Award for Literature from the Hawai'i Literary Arts Council. MacMillan also won awards for his teaching, and the literary journal he started in 1973, *The Hawai'i Review,* honored him recently with a double issue in his name that featured dozens of writers sharing stories about how he inspired their craft.

MacMillan had a sort of split literary personality, with his mainland published work on the one hand and his Hawai'i published writing on the other. The mainland work consists of his World War II novels and what he called his "cows and chainsaw" stories—all spun from his teenage experiences of farm life.

"For years they'd be in magazines like *Carolina Quarterly* and *Missouri Review.* And I would just write them and send them out, and they'd take. I have a... [new] collection that I'm playing around with. And then I have all these other stories, 20 or 30 or 40 of them lying around. So that's a whole literature for me, that upstate New York stuff, and I keep going back to it," said MacMillan, whose first book, *Light and Power* (University of Missouri Press, 1980), won the Associated Writing Programs Award for Short Fiction. His latest collection, *Our People,* was released in November 2008 by BkMk Press of the University of Missouri-Kansas City.

These stories are full of conflicts between fathers and sons, struggles to survive as small dairy and timber farmers in poor, rural American, and tangible longings for the often unnamable. An excerpt from "The Proper Axis" (*Our People*), reads, "He could not explain to his brother, who loved shooting birds with his .22, what it felt like in spring to walk through the woods with the chickadees following him, each one so close that he could see every minute detail of eyes and feathers and toothpick-thin legs. He could not explain how he felt that day when he walked along a gully one late winter morning and saw a buck twenty feet away, standing there steaming in the bright morning sunlight, the breath vapor shooting from its snout and the steam leaving his back like tongues of white fire."

MacMillan debuted as a novelist with *Blakely's Ark* (Berkeley Books, 1981), a dystopian science fiction novel about a catastrophic virus that decimates the human population. Next came *Proud Monster* (North Point Press, 1987), which evolved from a single short-short composed after a friend asked him, "Have you ever written a story of three pages or less?" The resulting piece, "The Unknown Soldier Passes," appeared in *TriQuarterly*, won a Pushcart Prize, and became the final chapter in the first book of his World War II trilogy.

"If *Proud Monster* is going to be called a novel, it's very experimental," MacMillan noted. "It's 70 short-shorts and over 500 characters. All are intended to be distinctly short stories rather than chapters in a book." The stories—poignant, stark, and masterfully (if excruciatingly) rendered—depict almost exclusively common people and their plights throughout Europe, since MacMillan perceived the war as so broad that it could only be told in a multiplicity of voices. Like all his writing, the prose is highly kinesthetic, anchoring the reader solidly in place with precise sensory details.

Second in the trilogy is *Orbit of Darkness* (Harcourt Brace Jovanovich, 1991), which moves beyond the short-shorts of *Proud Monster* to a series of 15 interrelated short stories about Auschwitz interspersed with 14 stand-alone stories. The final book in the series, and the most "novelistic," is *Village of a Million Spirits: A Novel of the Treblinka Uprising* (Steerforth Press, 1999 / Penguin Books, 2000). Without a doubt Village—favorably reviewed in the *New York Times Book Review, L.A. Times,* and *Publishers Weekly,* among others—garnered MacMillan the most widespread recognition to date, including the 2000 P.E.N. U.S.A.-West Fiction Award.

The prestige of a book like *Village,* however, didn't necessarily pave the way for MacMillan's short story collections or Hawai'i novels. For example, Steerforth Press knew about one of his "cows and chainsaws" short story manuscripts, but passed on it. Similarly, his New York literary agent Neil Olson, of Donadio & Olson, never handled MacMillan's short or regional fiction. "If he doesn't know what to do with something then he'll just say, 'Why don't you go ahead and do this one by yourself,'" shared MacMillan.

Although he was a self-identified WASP with no personal connection to the Holocaust, MacMillan nonetheless became obsessed with the subject. After completing the WW II trilogy, MacMillan finally declared the war "over" for him. Only then, after a 30-year residency, did he turn to his island home for subject matter.

When MacMillan wrote about Hawai'i, he tried to practice mindfulness. "If you're an outsider, you better represent it correctly. I've been here for years but I'm still a transplant. Most of my characters themselves are transplants," he stated. "The first thing I want to make sure is that I'm not being presumptuous."

The protagonist in MacMillan's first Hawai'i-themed novel, *The Red Wind* (Mutual Publishing, 1998), is a newcomer to the islands who apprentices with a master canoe builder.

"Kenika's attitude is my attitude," said MacMillan, "Be careful, show respect. He understands he's dealing with sacred cultural meanings and doesn't want to misrepresent them." In fact, there's a double meaning underlying the book: the Red Wind—a traditional Hawaiian canoe Kenika builds—rests in the hands of an immigrant craftsman, just as this novel of Hawai'i was crafted by an immigrant author.

A hefty 456 pages, *The Red Wind* has sold over 4,000 copies to date. In the novel's author's note, MacMillan wrote, "Although I have lived in Hawai'i since 1966, the idea of writing a book set in Hawai'i did not seriously enter my mind until the early 90s, and then only as a possibility. I had written books set in places I have never visited, about events I could have no firsthand knowledge of, had even written a science fiction novel set in the future. The other things I wrote, short stories mostly, were set in upstate New York, a place I had lived in only about seven years. But then at the back of mind I reasoned that more than a quarter of a century of familiarity with Hawai'i stood for something."

His short fiction collections *Exiles from Time* (1998), *Squid Eye* (1999), and *Ullambana* (2002) were un-agented and published by the very small Anoai Press. These stories often include dialogue in pidgin, a unique dialect of English evolved from Hawai'i's multi-cultural mix (Chinese, Japanese, Portuguese, Hawaiian, etc.), and explore issues of race, class, culture, coming of age, and every sort of relationship. Often MacMillan's work focuses more on a subtle shifting within or between characters than on some major plot device. An avid spear fisherman who lived in the seaside town of Kailua, he often used the ocean as a setting in his work.

MacMillan's novels *The Braid* and *The Seven Orchids* both feature protagonists who struggle with alcohol addiction, aimlessness, and self-annihilation. MacMillan characterized *The Braid* as "just a regular mainstream book" about "a boy growing up in, well, upstate...laughs...New York." The young man promises his dying mother that he will return her braid of hair to Hawai'i, where he was born. Upon arriving in Honolulu, the now homeless Adrian Branch meets a local runaway prostitute; and with her help, he searches for an appropriate spot to bury his mother's braid. Spanning two vastly different locales, this novel, more than any of MacMillan's other work, seems to bridge his "cows and chainsaws" motifs and his island themes.

While MacMillan's Hawai'i literature tends to feature male protagonists, *The Seven Orchids* was the first written entirely from a female's perspective, the cause of some discomfort for MacMillan. "It didn't make me feel strange to write from a woman's point of view in any of the World War II things. I felt perfectly natural with that. But in this book every word is from a woman's point of view. I would have to admit that it makes me uneasy, you know, just the existence of it. How can I know I'm right? How can I be absolutely sure?"

The *Seven Orchids*, at 46,000-something words, is more novella than novel and follows Danielle Baker, a half-hearted canoe paddler in self-imposed exile on the sleepy island of Moloka'i. After leaving her drug dealer boyfriend and life of constant partying on O'ahu, she moves to her father's fixer-upper property with her half-brother Kimo, taking her drug of choice—gin—along with her. She discovers an old, abandoned koa canoe with a tragic history and, together with a gang of other misfits, seeks redemption by returning it to the waves to race.

When he worked on a novel, MacMillan said he liked to know its beginning and maybe its middle, but not the end. He preferred the process of writing to direct what was going to happen next. Perhaps that's why, in his decades-long career, MacMillan never suffered from a bout of writer's block, always having more ideas than he could execute. "I have a whole list in my mind of really neat novels I never wrote because I never have the time," he quipped.

Unlike those with set writing schedules, MacMillan worked in spurts. He wouldn't write for weeks but then produced for several days on end. "If somebody told me I had to get up every morning and spend from six until nine writing, the first thing I would do would be to fail to meet that expectation," he noted. MacMillan didn't keep a schedule because the majority of his writing happened in his head—he thought about a piece for a month or two before it ever saw paper.

"By the time it's been so much beaten to death to the point that I'm already writing the first sentence, then I get out the spiral notebook. My hand just keeps on going until it's tired—three, four hours, or whatever—and I have 30, 40 handwritten pages. Then I let that rot for awhile. Then I go over it and I start putting stuff in the margins and go over it again until I can barely read my own handwriting." That's when MacMillan transferred his work into the computer to create the first printed draft.

What counsel did MacMillan give aspiring writers? "Know that what you're doing takes guts. Once you understand what you're doing, ignore outside influences...don't let anything distract you. It's just you and the universe you're creating. You have to trust yourself." Only at that point, he said, should you give your work to another for judgement.

"The other bit of advice I give to students is to be very suspicious of everybody's advice, including mine," he joked, seriously. The average M.F.A. writing program, he believed, often approaches teaching by hovering over the writer with the underlying message of 'Don't do that.' MacMillan tried to do the opposite, pushing students to cultivate unique voices. "I tell them that if they're doing something that looks like an anomaly or looks a little bit strange or a little bit whacked out, you know, or off to the side of what is done by other writers, you have two options: change it and make it conventional or take that apparent weakness and try and make it into a strength. The point is, you're the writer, this is how you do things, this is your stylistic fingerprint. My job is to figure out how to make that work, not to change it."

Finally, MacMillan encouraged: submit, submit, submit. "You can take a good short story and try and calculate what the probability would be that the chemistry would be right between you and the editor, and you might say it's one in 15 or something like that. So, get 30 stories in the mail. Guess what? You're going to get something accepted."

Following his own advice, MacMillan continued to work on his fiction even after he was diagnosed with stage-four pancreatic cancer in January 2008. He traveled to Johns Hopkins Hospital in Baltimore, Maryland, and according to a statement by his daughters, Laura Crago and Julia MacMillan, "The successful treatment he received there allowed him to spend the last eleven months with his brother in New Jersey, playing golf, taking Susan to theater productions and the Metropolitan Museum of Art, and spending time with all his family." With the story collection *Our People* and the novel *The Bone Hook* awaiting publication, he continued to write and edit throughout that summer.

MacMillan's death came a mere 20 days after his wife's, also from cancer. The daughters' statement affirmed, as anyone who knew them had witnessed, that the two "never liked to be apart for long." The 67-year-old author was held by his brother and two daughters as he passed on. They said, "True to his spirit throughout this battle he gripped our hands tightly to the end."

With a yet-to-be released novel and other still unpublished work waiting in the wings, MacMillan is likely to stay, as he proclaimed with relish, 'in the mail'—for many years to come.

The MacMillans were honored at four celebrations of their lives accompanied by a scattering of their ashes, at Kailua-Lanikai Beach, Hawai'i; Crested Butte, Colorado; East Atlantic Beach, Long Island; and Morningside Cemetery in Syracuse, New York. Contributions may be made to the Ian MacMillan Creative Writing Scholarship for Morris Central School, in care of: Judy Matson, District Clerk, Morris Central School, P.O. Box 40, 65 Main Street, Morris, NY 13808.

After her strange hiking companion had suddenly run off into the steep ravine and to the trail below, she stood alone in the mud-smelling updraft of wind and stared down the mountain at the marsh, at the buildings in Kailua, and beyond that the beach and the ocean horizon with huge, billowing clouds sitting on it, the thin white line left by a passing jet linking their tops. She pulled her water bottle out of her fanny pack and took a lukewarm slug. They'd been talking about the tree she stood under, and she had just thought that maybe he was someone she might like to talk to, and then he was gone. She looked down at herself, as if the reason might be evident there. Her running shoes and shins were spattered with mud. Now, away to the left, he appeared walking on the trail, looking like someone who remembered leaving a pot of boiling water on a stove. He stopped, one hand on his head, pulled something out of his pocket—a cell phone—opened it, stared, snapped it shut, and went on around some brush and out of sight. "What was that about?" she whispered, putting the water bottle back. Her right foot was wet and sticky inside her running shoe. There was a sudden lull in the wind, so that she thought she could hear a kind of ticking percolation in the mulch under her feet, and in the distance she heard the hum of traffic on the Pali Highway, late-morning commuters on their way to Honolulu.

She turned and looked at the breadfruit tree, its leaf mulch dark and glistening. It was probably more than a hundred years old, but small, the harsh upland weather having stunted it, leaving only the huge lower leaves intact, looking like cartoon hands with too many fingers. She had seen the sparse canopy from the trail about seventy yards below and told the others that she'd catch them later. She climbed up a narrow and steep dry ravine, and when she was halfway there, she was aware that the guy, whose name was Something Lindross, a strange first name, was following her. He was the guy who, earlier, had lagged back and, when he thought no one was looking, collected stones and threw them at trees and rocks, which made her wonder. So when she climbed up that ravine, she stopped and looked back at him *watch out* and realized that he was no threat because of the flustered look on his face, as if he was afraid of getting lost.

They kept hiking, climbing over black basalt boulders, she a little self-conscious about his being behind her, and came to the tree. When he got there, breathing heavily, she said it was odd that a breadfruit tree would be in this remote place, and he'd said, uh, yeah. He'd pushed sandy blonde hair up from his forehead, and she saw that his eyes were brown, kind of a weird combination considering the hair. Then she'd said, "They don't seed, so it has to have been planted here, but the place isn't really habitable, which is strange. You couldn't build a fire here, or even a thatch house."

"Okay," he said. "Uh, but wait a minute. Somebody planted it?" He turned and looked down the flanks of the mountain, thinking. There was a thick, white column of rain moving in, to the left. It would miss them.

"It's *Artocarpus altilis*," she said, and there his face went strange. He stared at her, then at the tree, and then did a jerky turn, his hand on his head.

"But," he said.

"I mean, that's its name?" she said, somewhat uncertainly. He wasn't listening. He was looking back down the ravine.

"I hafta–" he said, and then stumbled into the ravine, stopped, turned and gestured as if to speak again, and then went on out of sight.

Standing there buffeted by the wind, she had wondered what she could have said that would set him off like that. Some obscure phobia about Latin? Latinitus, or Latinophobia? Or perhaps the use of the Latin name had triggered his memory of the boiling water on the stove.

When she got back to the trail, she had two options: catch up with the others on the trail or go home, like that strange guy. Jerry Leonardo and his brother, and two other girls, kind of jovial and wild girls, were probably easy to catch up with because they were slow, but she wasn't sure about Jerry Leonardo, or his brother Mike. Jerry had arranged this hike, but they brought booze with them, and "a surprise" as he had put it, probably dope of some sort. Which meant that the brothers were trying to arrange an orgy. They wore backpacks that were rather large, and that had made her wonder. When she considered catching up with them, visualizing what they were probably planning *don't do it* came across, so she went the other way, walking fast because she felt strange being alone.

When she got to the parking area, the traffic sweeping by on the curve down toward Castle Junction, she saw her moped by itself next to the vacant spot left by Something Lindross. She made her way across the lot, looking down at bottle caps and cigarette butts, one scraped-up disk reflecting blue-green sunlight, and got on and started the moped, then waited for a break in the traffic. The break came accompanied by woofers in a Civic that vibrated her ribs and pulsed in her head, and she pulled out, running over something yellow. A large screwdriver *get it get the screwdriver* so she pulled over into the grass, walked back up the little ramp, picked it up, and put it in the compartment under her seat. Almost brand new. You never knew when you'd need a screwdriver.

He did not want to run anyone over, or dent a fender. He did not want to get a ticket. He held the wheel, made it to the first light in Kailua, waited until his turn, and went around to his building and parked the car on the street. "Arti—" he whispered, "arti-something," and got out and walked between the line of doors and the hollow-tile wall above which loomed wires, tan, barrel-shaped condensers, huge insulators, all producing that hum he always thought over-electrified his brain. He unlocked the door and went in, the air moldy and humid. The phone blinked, his sister again. He sighed, picked it up, and poked the button. "It's Sherry. Listen, clown, interest rates are going up, time's wasting, and you've got to make up your fucking mind okay?" Click.

"Breadfruit," he said, looking around at the mounds of junk mail and magazines and different papers in piles on the coffee table and on the floor under and around it, and on the couch. He looked at the door to his mother's room. Maybe that faint odor was gone. He went to the kitchen and looked out through the sliding glass door. The orchids were okay. There were about fifty of them, crowding the little back patio, so that you had to work your way around them to get to the washing machine and dryer. He'd water them later.

He went back to the door to his mother's room. Twenty-three, he thought, and afraid of a room. He opened the door, his hand shaking a little, and reached around and turned on the light so that the room was bathed in the dull yellow glow of the dusty ceiling bulb. He half expected to see an unmade bed, but he'd gotten rid of that bed, and all that was left was the metal frame hovering over a square of dust and bits of paper and pennies, a few peanut shells and a paper clip. He put his head in and sniffed—okay, but then, the hint of it was still there, that suggestion of ripening to the point of decomposition. It was still there, he was sure. Three and a half, no, four weeks now, and it was still there.

He took a deep breath and went in, to the closet. On the top shelf was the box, her jewelry box, an ornate black Chinese thing with bits of mother-of-pearl in the shape of swans inset in the lacquered wood. It felt sticky because of the humidity. He took the box to the kitchen table, letting his breath out as he went. He felt watched. He got up and turned off her light and closed the door.

It was in a small leather pouch. He found it, knew by the weight that it was in there. He slid it out—a lump of gold in a rough circle, with the Spanish seal from centuries ago impressed in the middle, slightly offset from the lumpy edge. The supposed value of a doubloon of this sort was around fifteen thousand dollars, but his sister blew that off. "That's bullshit, a couple thou," she'd said. "It's the apartment that's worth the bucks. Sell the coin and give me half plus proof that you're not screwing me okay? Meanwhile, let's work on selling the unit, before the bottom drops out of the market."

He put the coin back in the pouch and the pouch in the box. Next was the envelope, and the thought of that made him begin to sweat, because he didn't know where it was, or if it even still existed, if, in the confusion after she died he had thrown it away without knowing what it was. He pictured handfuls of magazines and junk mail he'd filled garbage bags with and suspected it had gone out with those. And if he hadn't thrown it away, then maybe his mother's friend Natalie Duncan had. The lady had helped his mother "arrange her affairs" while she was sick. Natalie Duncan was a real estate dealer and worked a lot with banks and knew the rules for this stuff, and she was helpful even though he didn't like her very much. She was sweet to the point of ridiculousness, and his mother's dying had seemed to make her almost ghoulishly sweet. He wasn't sure that this lady's advice was that great either. She suggested early on that his mother sell the unit and rent, and then invest the profits, without considering the tax consequences of not using the money to buy another property. Or maybe he was wrong about that, he didn't know. But after his mother died, she stopped calling and didn't visit. But then, why would she? he wondered. She and her husband Ray still did invite him to dinner at restaurants, though. Ray was a good guy and always seemed concerned about the situation, and because he was an investment counselor, he would have been the better advisor.

He probably wasn't thinking straight when he started clearing that stuff out. He had done well, he thought, in taking care of her while she was dying, taking her to her appointments, keeping her hopes up, discussing the results of medical tests. He'd kept the orchids watered, and brought in ones that were blooming to put by her bedside. Then he'd been invited by one of his old volunteer coaches at the University to attend a baseball camp for kids on Maui, to teach them pitching techniques, and although he was out of college and wasn't playing, they thought that he'd be a good fit for the kids. He told his mother about it and told her that he wouldn't go, but she urged him to go, that their neighbor Millie Leong would check on her. So he rearranged some of his work hours and went.

He had called from Maui when he got there, and she was all right, she said. He didn't need to use up minutes on his phone; just have fun. So he did, and when he got home, he found his mother in her bed, eyes closed and somewhat sunken, little black ants crawling around on the sheet, and the fan faintly riffling the point of the blue kerchief she wore. She had been dead as long as thirty or more hours, the paramedics had told him, and that was when he realized what he'd been smelling from the moment he walked in: her beginning to turn.

The problem was that Millie Leong had checked at first, but his mother had told her not to change her plans over this, and so Millie had visited her family on the Leeward side, and after that had either assumed he was back or gone according to his mother's instructions and not worried about her. So he had assumed everything was all right while he showed the kids the proper stances, the form of a pitch. He was wrong, and that image of her, lying there with the fan aimed at her, that blue kerchief around her head because of the sparseness of her hair, that look of haunted questioning on her face, followed him everywhere. He'd never believed in ghosts, but now was watched by one.

He thought of turning the computer on and shuddered. With nothing to do in his free time after the little beach ceremony where they put her ashes in the water at Lanikai, he took to playing solitaire obsessively on the computer. Like the apartment, his computer was full of too much shit—so much that he had no access to the net. Any time he tried to use it, the machine would think, then freeze, so solitaire was all that was left. He had begun putting too much stock in the results, so that if he couldn't win out in three tries, he determined that he would have a bad day, or week, or, sometimes, a bad life.

It was four o'clock. He went outside to the little lanai and picked up the short hose hitched to the spout, and with the spray on fine, watered the orchids. More than ten of them were in full bloom, and he thought briefly of putting one on the table by her bed and then shook his head. They were blooming for nobody. He had to look for the envelope, but didn't want to—the room was full of his mother, all her clothes, all the family photos, her medicines, magazines, the little TV she watched, the dusty boxes of junk she'd saved, including incompetent sculptures he and his sister had done in school. The only stuff that had been removed was her good jewelry, which his sister took; a valuable poi-pounder, which his sister took; a collection of antique bone fishhooks, which his sister took. Because the lacquered box had costume jewelry in it, she had opened it, looked in, and said, "Just shit," and pushed it away. She'd apparently forgotten the doubloon, and by extension, the envelope. In the lacquered box there were, in the bottom tray, a few more hooks on chains, which she had also missed.

He got an idea. That girl who named the tree in Latin, Terry Something, like Almeida or Olmeda or whatever, the one who always looked wary, who backed away whenever you stepped close, who seemed always mentally occupied somewhere else. Maybe she knew more: how long does a breadfruit tree live? Would a person in his right mind ever decide to use one as a marker? He finished the watering and went to the phone. One of the other girls had given him Terry's number before the hike. Just a safety measure should anyone become lost. He tried to figure out what to say, and then dialed the number. It rang a while, then, "Hi, this is Terry. Leave a message."

The traffic was a mess approaching the intersection at the hospital, and she had to stand straddling the machine and wait for it to inch ahead, listening to whistles and catcalls *ignore them* until she was able to skirt along the right toward the highway that led to Keolu Drive. Then she buzzed over the hill to the stretch between Olomana Mountain on the right and the broad panorama of Kailua and the ocean on her left. La'au Lane was a cul-de-sac off Akamai Street, and as she approached the house she shared with her brother Derek, she felt that old warm rush of embarrassment. Their place had become an eyesore with cars, either stolen or acquired legally, littering the street, the lawn, the formerly grassy area next to the house, and the back yard. Her parents were in Vegas, her father trying a job at a casino. They left the job of paying the mortgage and the other bills to her and Derek, which meant that it was her job. Her father was also a car freak, so he would not only say nothing about the parking lot their place had become but would probably roll up his sleeves to help, and her mother would say nothing as long as the TV was on. But she still had her hideaway, her room. She kept it meticulously clean no matter how ratty and cluttered the rest of the house had become.

As she slowed the moped down, she saw Billy Neal's car, and growled with frustration. Just getting past him was a challenge. He was an old friend of Derek's, hapa, the mysterious half no concern of hers, and was always trying to get close to her *no way* and she considered sneaking in the back door, but they were apparently inside. She got the screwdriver out of the compartment.

She went to the front where it smelled of gasoline and oil, and opened the door. On the living room floor, with the rug rolled back and a paint-spotted tarp in its place, stood an enormous Harley-Davidson chopper without its handlebars, the blue gas tank's sheen marked by fingerprints, the chrome works underneath dully glinting with oil. Beers popped in the kitchen, and out they came.

"What's this?" she asked, gesturing with the screwdriver.

"Merry Terry," Billy Neal said.

"Just some work for a friend," Derek said.

There was a flat look on his face *don't ask* and Billy started looking at her that way she hated.

"Terry," he said. "I get my check—get chance?"

"No."

"What's the screwdriver for?"

She looked at it. "I'm repairing my watch," she said, and went to her door.

"Fuck," Billy said to Derek. "Get one mout' ah, yoa sistah?"

"Whatever," Derek said, looking at the chopper. "C'mon, let's keep at it."

"I make nice alla time," Billy said. "What I get? Pretty soon I get extreme mento whatevahs. Stress ah?"

"You'll be all right," she said, and unlocked the door and went into her room while behind her, Billy said, "I ask you out how many fricken times? Dis jus' unfair." She closed the door and threw the bolt, and locked the little twist lock in the handle, hearing him carry on: "I one nice guy you know. You'll see. We—" He was cut off by the scream of some electric tool, a Dremel maybe. It sounded like they had to erase the identity of the Harley. So now she lived in a chop shop.

Inside the room she felt the pressure drop. She thought of it as the room of her secret little insanities, and she kept it very neat. There she had her bed, dresser, bookshelves, and her desk, on which was her Hewlett Packard rig. There was a nice Costco rug and framed photos she took of flowers, her favorite the night-blooming Cereus, *Selenicereus grandiflorus*, a huge flower with white petals resembling pigeon's feathers, and a yellow stamen. It bloomed at sundown and wilted the next morning.

Everybody had their little insanities, and all you needed to do was balance them, manage them properly. There were three for her, the first in the drawer in which she now placed the screwdriver: the kit, four unopened boxes holding cold medicine, and a pint flask of Cutty Sark Scotch. The kit had been in the drawer now six years. At first, when she was seventeen, it had frightened and obsessed her, because the means to get out of it all was always there, seeming to glow, or pulse, every time she opened the drawer. But over the years it had become so familiar, so much a simple accoutrement of the room that it now gave her a strange comfort, those boxes all grouped together next to the green bottle. It meant that she always held the keys to her own situation, so that it seemed like no more than a savings account or an insurance policy.

Now there was a screwdriver in the drawer with the kit, a yellow transparent handle with the fuzzy post inside. She didn't know why she'd picked it up, but it felt right that it was there.

The reason for the kit was the voice, her second insanity. The voice was that of a child. When she was seventeen, her boyfriend, who was twenty-five, got her pregnant. He was a college student majoring in art, and the more he pleaded with her to get rid of it, that he couldn't fit a child into his life, the more her body told her to keep it. He told her that no matter what happened, whether they were together or not, he could not see how he could assimilate a child into his life. The pleading got annoying, and she told him she was keeping it and dumped him. But he kept calling her, coming by to see her to advance his argument. She had to understand, he told her. The very existence of this child could not fit his plans and she was being selfish. For him, it would always be there and he would somehow be responsible and he could not fit that in. And it would compromise his inspiration. Every work of art he tried to produce would be haunted by this child, and he just could not see how he could live like that.

At the beginning of the second trimester, she lost it. The memory of this was a blur, of her mother comforting her as they drove to Castle Hospital, of hearing the baby was lost, the short stay at the hospital. But it was not over. In her dreams or in her half-sleep a baby cried, and it lasted so long that the crying became gurgling and soft cooing, and then words, the ghost baby's first words. It was a girl, and it grew up to become a wise child, an advisor to her, who warned her in sticky situations, who was always there and who would interject terse advice in that high, soft voice. She had assembled the kit when she was seventeen and the crying began. Now, after six years, the child commented on the kit only rarely *you don't need that* and she had been so much a part of Terry's life that she became alarmed if three or four hours passed without any warnings, any two- or three-word comments, or advice.

She briefly saw a counselor about this, a man whose job it was to help her out and give suggestions about the management of her life. He told her that the voice was something she herself had invented *not* and that she herself should just turn it off. The mind compensates for trauma. When she told him she really did hear it and had not invented it, he became frustrated; something as trivial as this voice should just be bagged and thrown out if she were to advance at all. Didn't she see that? She was advancing, she told him, but the voice advanced with her. The man just snorted and said that he did not believe in voices, and that half the time when someone was arrested for murder, the first thing that person said was, "I heard voices," and perhaps she had bought into that since she'd heard it so much on TV. No, she said, this one is real. The man ignored her and tried to change the subject.

The third little insanity was a saying that she found at Daiei in the dollar section of Asian import stuff. She had wandered in there one day to buy some small office supplies for herself and found memo pads and plastic boxes with sayings on them, all of them ungrammatical and startlingly nonsensical because apparently, the manufacturers in Japan didn't have English speakers to help them write sayings or label boxes logically. There was a box called "The New Memory Pot," and one called "The Million Range Pack," and another with pictures of vegetables on it over which was written "Quite Life and Tasty Vegetable." There was a "Pure" box, "This case is designed for arrangement of anything goods," and the "Folca" box, a small but elaborate tri-fold plastic box with tiny compartments intended, she thought, for little pieces of jewelry. The saying on the orange cover read, "If it always has Folca an important thing will not forget." And notepads: there was one that had printed on the plastic cover, "It's true love we're making—as something to lost for all time," and another that said, "This notebook is excellent quality and royal to learn—put pen to this paper." She began going to Daiei just to look at these objects, until she came across a memo pad with the following on the top of each page: "Do the dream dance with your body on."

It had made her laugh, but when she reread it a number of times, she began to see secret meanings in the statement that somehow applied to her. For days the child's voice was nearly mute but for one-word comments, as if the wise six-year-old were carefully considering the meanings herself, those short comments blurted out in distracted asides. Terry decided to put the statement on the screen of her computer, superimposed on her portrait of the Mokulua Islands baking in the sun off Lanikai. Just as she began typing, she paused *yes, it's for us* and took a breath, wondering why it had taken the child so long to consider, and finally, approve of it. After that, the statement or parts of it became incantations or mantras, reference points for both of them, so that when she felt good, even at work, she was doing the dream dance and her body was on, or if someone asked her out and she thought about it, the voice would whisper *don't your body's not on* and Terry would politely decline.

She could never tell anyone of these insanities, just as she knew others, even the two out there hammering and cursing and popping beers, couldn't tell of their little insanities. You managed them, that was all.

Five o'clock. She would change her muddy shoes and get ready to go to Subway for dinner. She went there four times a week and ate a six-inch spicy Italian sub. She grabbed her fanny pack and opened it, took out her cell. There was a message. Hm. She pressed "1" and waited for it.

Nothing. She was about to close it when she heard, "Uh," then more silence. Then, "Uh, this is Emil, remember, the guy who vanished up above the trail today?" Silence. "I mean, uh, I had a question for you. It has to do with the tree, and I wanted—" Silence. "Uh, wait. This is ridiculous. Maybe if you just called. I mean if you want. Whatever. My number—" She considered calling *he's okay* and decided to go ahead.

He heard her unlocking her door just as Derek went to the can, and she came out of the room in different clothes, jeans and T-shirt, walked right past him without saying anything. "Terry babes," he said. "I hurteen fo' you."

Out she went, the screen door slapping shut behind her. He snorted, prickling with that faint rage that the bitch's in-your-face rejection caused whenever she blew him off. He went to the front door and watched as she went down the lane between two junk cars and raised her leg and lowered her business district onto the moped seat, and he thought, anything, whatever it takes. He had to. It was one fucken crime against humanity that she was such a bitch. She didn't have any idea what she did to him, how she drove him nuts with that awful want, and he didn't need that much out of life. Not really. Derek came out of the can and went into the kitchen. Billy watched him fiddling with the microwave.

Yeah, Billy could read her. She played shy but was a secret slut, the quiet, sweet kind who took vibrators to bed with her and dreamed of getting the big one from somebody like Billy, but couldn't cross that line. Who the fuck cared about the Harley? Fix the goddam thing up for chump change for another guy who stole it? He thought they'd be over that petty shit by now. In fact, it was way more fun when he and Derek worked for chump change at the golf course. They could play nines late in the day if they felt like it, and life was easy.

Derek was pawing around in the freezer. Billy moved toward the kitchen, to her door. He tried the handle but it was locked. Shit, a credit card would open that—the cheesy hollow-core piece of shit. He got an idea. He pulled his keys out, and on the chain was a thumb drive. Derek told him that she was good with computers—maybe chicks who needed it got good at computers, he didn't know, but he was better. He would sneak into her room and load a cool porn picture on her screen. It was easy, and she'd know who did it. It would be a message. She would sit there and stare at the picture, get all hot. He would be communicating with her—see, I got one of those too, just as big, you shy little slut. You like some? It was either that or a goddam date-rape pill as far as he was concerned.

"Pizza," Derek called.

"Cool," he said. He had to get out of here soon. His boss would have shit for him to do tonight. Saturday night in Waikīkī was boogie-time—deliveries and collections, small time for now, but if he played his cards right, he'd be wallowing in some serious cash pretty soon.

The pizza was DiGiorno's. Looking at Derek, he shook his head. Still fucking with vehicles. Billy worked for a high roller, and he was slumming by hanging out with him. Derek was so bush league.

He was ten minutes early at the Subway. So he stood there and watched cars jockeying for spaces in the lot, the Saturday afternoon rush when people picked up the beer and chips and stuff for their barbecues, while Saturday nights he watched TV and played solitaire. Sunday nights too, except that this Sunday he was invited out by the Duncans, who were more or less taking care of him that way since his mother died. Mrs. Duncan would probably have more advice about what to do with the unit.

He reached into his pocket and felt the little leather pouch that held the doubloon. He was nervous about trying to make this Terry Something believe him. It had to be like a presentation, with a full–

A moped came in behind a black Hummer. She maneuvered around it and pulled up in front of the Subway, considered where she ought to park it. She chose the striped delivery area near Subway, but put the moped at the edge. She looked around, saw him, and got off. She looked with it, competent and smart. Why was that? Something about the pleasing compactness of her body, the smoothness of her movements. Then he shook his head. This is not about sex, stupid, he thought. It's about doubloons. He stepped away from the Subway window and nodded to her.

"Okay," she said. "Something about a tree."

"Yeah," he said. "But it's complicated."

She looked away. She looked back at her moped, thinking, or listening to someone else.

"Uh, I need to explain?" he said.

"Okay," she said. "I'm hungry."

They went inside. At the counter, the guy looked at her and started making a six-inch. Then he saw Emil and said, "And what will you have?"

"Uh, make it the same." The guy kept working. Emil watched, making sure that the correct number of slices of this and that went on. If you didn't watch, you'd get short salamied. Or short cheesed.

When he was finished and they paid, she looked around. There were only three tables, and she led him to the little one by the door. Sitting down across from her, he looked at his sandwich. "So this one is good? I noticed you didn't even tell him what to put on it."

"It's what I get," she said.

This, he thought, was really awkward, but the little bit of stage fright he felt about explaining all of this vanished. She just concentrated on her sandwich. Almost like he wasn't there, so he picked up his and took a bite.

"So'd you finish the hike?" he asked.

"No," she said. "What was the surprise he said he had?"

"I don't know. I don't know him that well. In fact, I don't even know why he invited me."

"So are you in college?"

He picked up a napkin and wiped his mouth. A fat man holding a cell phone to his ear came in, walked past their table saying, "Nineteen. I mean it's not like—"

Terry seemed fascinated by the man, holding her sandwich, her face stilled in mid-chew.

"Yeah, I was in college. Two years, then two off, then I was going back, but there were, uh, well, what you call circumstances?"

"Two years?"

"College?"

"Oh, yes, college," she said.

"Well, I was like, on the baseball team? I pitched? Mostly relief, but that's still hard."

He wiped his mouth again and explained the whole thing: college, baseball, his mother's death. When he was finished she stopped chewing. "I'm really sorry about your mother," she said.

"Well, yeah, it's—"

She started eating again. He reached into his pocket and drew out the leather pouch and put it on the table. She looked at it, chewing. He held the bottom end and pulled it back, leaving the strange coin there. She swallowed and squinted at it.

"This is a Spanish doubloon," he said. "It belonged to my great great—well, let's say a few greats—grandfather, who was a sailor who was here in the nineteenth century. This is gonna sound like some movie with whatsisname, but—"

"The word 'doubloon' already did it. Aye, matey."

"I know. Anyway, he hid a bunch of doubloons along with a bunch of Hawaiian artifacts in a cave somewhere, most likely on the Windward side. This is where the tree comes in. He had a bunch of coordinates and distances from what he put down as *Artocarpus altilis*, which he planted, or so the story goes. The information is on some old ratty pieces of paper we have in an envelope somewhere at our place, I mean my place I guess it would be now, because—"

He pictured her in the bed. He pictured the half-full bottle of water on the table, and the orchid he had left there, the breeze from the fan moving the kerchief. So she had water when she—

"So why didn't anybody look for this tree before?" she asked.

"The tree. The paper didn't say anything about where the tree was, only that everything is such and such a distance from the tree."

"That tree was planted," she said, "because the Hawaiian breadfruit doesn't self- seed. The area doesn't look to me like one anybody would choose to live in, because it's too windy."

"But then the tree he mentions could have been planted anywhere. That's the problem. This might not be the one."

"So you don't know for sure it was the Windward side."

"No, only that he lived on the Windward side."

"Which means if he buried this stuff, he'd have buried it on this side. Nobody would haul Hawaiian artifacts over the Pali to hide them on the Honolulu side. There was only a trail there back then."

"Yeah." She stared again at the coin.

"What else?" he said. "The great whatever of mine hiked a lot on the slopes between Olomana and the Ko'olaus, because he had a thing for botany and collecting stuff. He did a lot of drawings of plants. We have some."

"So what's a doubloon worth?"

"Five to fifteen thousand dollars, according to my mother. It's the age and design. Not all are worth that, but she said this one is."

She picked it up and looked at it. "So it's like, a rare coin. How many of these did he supposedly hide?"

"Three hundred and six," he said. Her eyes went wide there.

"You have a pen?" she asked.

"I already did it. It's around one and a half million at the low to four and a half at the high."

"And the artifacts? What were they?"

"Wood images, you know, god and goddess statues, stone things, fishhooks, all that. The old papers list them. Anyway, he got killed by somebody, probably over this stuff, and the only description of where it is comes down to what's in the envelope. I don't know what my mother did with it."

Terry looked at the coin again, studying it. So now what? He watched her as she looked, turning it over and squinting. "So you see planting this tree as a good idea for a marker?" he asked. Lame question, but he wanted to keep the conversation going.

"Well, anybody interested in botany might think of it as a good marker," she said. "But it's sort of iffy, assuming that it would grow. Unless he stayed around to make sure that it did." She paused, again thinking, and then looked at him with the strange, guarded expression. "So why me? I mean, why'd you ask me about this?"

He flushed. Now he wasn't sure. Of course he could have figured this out by himself, but for one reason—the apartment, that's what it was. He couldn't deal with it. And he supposed he couldn't really tell her about it either. Just clean it up and find the stupid envelope, idiot.

"Well," he said, "maybe it's nothing you—no, I mean I guess I need—" He couldn't figure out how to put it. "Okay, let's see. How you fit in is the—" No, Latin had nothing to do with it.

"Can I suggest something?" she asked. "Something tells me your body's not—no, I mean you're not sure what you want. So let's just say if you think of something, I can help."

"Well, thanks."

"But that doesn't really make anything clear. So what was the great whatever's name?"

"Uh, Emiliano Gamez, uh, the last name with an A instead of an O."

"Hey," she said, seeming to brighten up. "Isn't that your name?"

He flushed again. "Uh, I call myself Emilio. I mean my name's Emiliano, but you know, it's sort of awkward. It's like, I have four names coming from that one, Emiliano, Emilio—"

She wasn't listening. She was staring into a weird middle distance, thinking. "Wait," she said. She continued staring. "Was this guy famous or something?"

"Well, his murder was, a little," he said. "And Emil, and then just Em. That's four."

"I've read the name somewhere. Not in connection with a murder though. If anything, it was botany." She thought again, then shook her head. "Nope. And your last name—Lindross. That's a strange—" She waved her hands around. "Combination?"

"Yeah, I don't have a clue what my parents were thinking. They have regular names. I mean, his is Doug, hers is Maile, I mean, or was Maile, and Lindross is kind of a regular old name, right? But anyway, people just refer to me as Em."

"That's not it, though," she said.

"Em's not it?"

"No, there's something else."

What did that mean? Then he thought he knew. Okay, so he had to tell her. Maybe he should. "Okay, I can't go through my mother's stuff. I don't know what to do with her clothes, and with all the junk in the place. I mean, junk mail, stuff from banks, legal stuff, medical bills. It's letters from friends, it's magazines, and books, and sympathy cards, and it's notes on this and that. What do I do about the will? What do I do about my sister, who wants to sell the place now and where do I go if we sell it? What about the rusty old Vanagon full of more crap that's in the parking space for the apartment, so I have to look for parking on the street? What about, well, what about anything? I go in there and I can't do anything about it. I thought—"

She stared at him. She looked at the coin, then out the window. Boys walked by. Cars jockeyed for spaces.

"I can help if you want," she said. "I mean if you need some kind of help cleaning up and all." Then she paused, looking down at his hands on the table. He watched her looking at his hands until he thought he should pull them away. Then she looked up at him. "What is a split-fingered fastball?"

He held his hand up, and inside his crooked fingers was an imaginary baseball.

He sat by the pool going over a portfolio, jotted "small cap" in a margin, and put the portfolio down. He couldn't concentrate. He didn't like it. He didn't like a lot of things she did, but this he didn't like at all. He got up from the chair and went into the kitchen. The pictures were on the counter, blown up but only partially readable. He leaned over and read the old fashioned script: "Cave—no bones." After that it said, "Use—" and there the letters seemed nonsensical. "A" something, followed by "A" something else. Natalie came out of the bathroom and down the hall looking at her watch.

"Gotta go," she said. "I'll be back at four." She looked out the kitchen window. The sound of hacking in dirt came in through it. It was their man, George Curley, hidden behind some ti plants.

"What's the Credible Hulk doing out there?" she asked.

"Weeding," he said. "You told him to weed, and he weeds."

"This is micro-weeding. I can't find any in the yard. It's the pool I want him to clean."

"He did that."

"Ah," she said.

"So what are these for?" he asked, pointing at the pictures. He looked at his watch. He had to leave soon, too. Mondays were busy at the office.

"Oh that's just interesting. A buried treasure, okay? We've been hearing about it for twenty-five years, remember? It's just an old story that's more myth than anything else."

"Does it have something to do with Em's mentioning finding a tree last night? That thing about hiking and a tree?"

"It reminded me that I took the pictures," she said. "Maile showed them to me."

"What's the point in taking pictures of it?"

"There is no point. It's just interesting, that's all. Look, I've gotta help Darlene show this house, okay?"

"Okay."

"And the Hulk," she said. "When he's done, tell him I left an address on his windshield. It's a lawn job."

"His name is George," he said.

"Well I call him the Hulk. It's a term of endearment."

"Okay."

She went out of the kitchen and left. He stood there, then leaned over again to study the pictures. Under the unreadable words beginning with what looked like the letter A were some strange numbers and letters: something illegible followed by "yds No.," to another illegible number followed by "yds. E," then another couple words he couldn't read. The second and third photos were lists: "Image—kou, 22, image, kou, 25," and the list went on through spears, clubs, and ended with "Bone Fishing Hooks." After that was written "specie—8's—306." All of this was apparently in some cave somewhere, those coordinates connected with the double-A combination of words that were written in a script that made them hard to interpret.

He went back twenty years to when his two boys were three and five and Emilio was three and his sister was four and they played together, and Maile Lindross, so pretty and so perfect with the children, watched them play in the inflatable pool while Natalie played tennis at the Racquet Club, and Emilio—nice, quiet kid, playing with the boys and his sister while Maile watched, and it had seemed to him so perfect, that he had wished his own wife had those natural instincts.

Those days they lived next to each other in little old tract houses in Keolu Hills, back when Kailua town was more of a dusty country town. After that, after Doug Lindross left Maile and the kids, he and Natalie moved to the Ku'ulei tract to a bigger house a long block from the beach, and now it's worth two million dollars, he thought—not that that would satisfy her. While the Lindross family, what was left of it, bought a horrible little two-bedroom dump next to an electrical station in town and it had worried him, he had lost sleep over Maile's having to cope with all that all those years, while his boys went to Punahou and then college on the mainland, a hundred thousand a year it cost, but they had the money, not that it satisfied her. He had reacted, inside, with a suspicious excess of sorrow upon hearing of her death, and it made him wonder, made him imagine a life where he had married Maile rather than Natalie, and he realized that he had secretly imagined this alternate life for a long time, just idle fantasizing, until in retrospect, he had realized that it was not idle; it was real, maybe more real than the life he did live, as if what seemed idle or silly in the back of his mind was really more than it seemed once the source of that fantasy was removed, making any possible reality impossible, and he was left leaning over a counter staring at digital photographs.

He wondered what Natalie was up to now, probably cashing in on this if she could, because the poor kid mentioned a tree, not that all the money they had was enough for her. And now Emilio, who'd had to drop out of college and stop playing baseball, had to deal by himself with the whole thing, his sister in LA, and even his former friends, the boys, living the high life in California, didn't have any interest in him any more because what selfish, rich boy would want to associate with a kid who lived in a dump like that? But Ray would have preferred living even there, with her, than in the Taj Mahal with Natalie. If he could have had a second chance he would have lived in a pup-tent on the beach in Mokulēʻia with her. He would have, no question.

You have to forget Maile, he thought. Look at your yard, your maintenance man hacking away at weeds, your flat-screen TV, your Lexus, look at your clients' accounts, at your boys living it up on the mainland, at your unit in Kona, at all your money, not that it really satisfies her.

So they were surfing. The Harley sat on the tarp oozing oil spots, a cockroach hearing the door open scuttled around with a metallic ticking in the bottom of a Bud can, the toilet seat was up, and the dishes weren't washed. She went to her room, thinking about Emilio's strange story, about whatever it might have been that made him call her. The usual motive was sleazy, but with him she wasn't sure *he's okay, he is* because of that confused look on his face, as if he could have been talking to a counselor or a priest. He seemed like a good guy, a goofy, sandy-haired guy who was most of the time a step behind whatever was going on.

The way they'd left things on Saturday, standing out there in front of the Subway, was that Terry would find all she could on her computer about Emiliano Gamez, and doubloons, and wooden statues. They couldn't email because his computer had some problem, so they'd have to meet again, and there she had paused, right when he asked if she'd be willing to help go through stuff some evening soon, paused, and then *go ahead, he's okay* told him she'd stop by on Tuesday evening, maybe for a couple hours. Weekdays were out. For her Sunday was out. She had to work—orders, bookkeeping, and phone calls all day at the Plant and Garden Warehouse. She saved all her money because she wanted to go to college to study botany. He had to work too, as a self-employed gardener and landscaper, which was strange, she thought, because it was just what she would have liked to do if she had the skills and the brawn. He was installing a long and elaborate series of steps at a house in Maunawili, and if he was to do anything about doubloons, or images, or any of that, it would have to be in a week or two. He'd just finished a big project in Lanikai that involved moving a lot of rocks and dirt.

She turned on the computer. Waited. Then came the Mokes, a picture she took, with the superimposed saying: Do the dream dance with your body on. She stared at it. Then came the same question she asked in her mind every time she turned the computer on. Is life a dream dance? Or if it is, you probably wouldn't want to do it with your body off. Off meant, maybe, like a lamp. On meant like with electricity, which—

Oh well. She pulled up Word, and tried to recall everything he said, and set it up:

Cave has no bones.

1. He had said that the old paper said that. [Removes any fear of disturbing spirits, Hawaiian stuff. Or seemingly.]

2. Said he remembered that one direction was 172 yards true north [which means downslope and then across the trail. Was there a trail in old days? Would terrain change when trail was made enough to alter measurement?]

3. The *Artocarpus altilis*. start point [duh]

4. Cave has to be big because of all the wooden statues [what about termites after 100 years—check if termites exist at that altitude]

5. Look great great g. up [pirate, or what?]

6. 15,000 per doubloon is a stretch. Need pic. of this.

7. Said E. Gamez drew botanicals—maybe where I heard of him. Have to see some.

8. What are wooden statues and bone hooks and spears worth? Check Ebay. What is 'bag of hooks'?

9. What about state archives? Would there be a record of the murder? [probably]

10. How different were things in 18—? Did that many haoles live on Windward side? Would you need help to bury all this stuff? How far was cave from house?

11. Is this a good idea?

12. Is writing all this down sick or anal or

She deleted numbers eleven and twelve. She printed the sheet and saved the list. She opened the drawer. The screwdriver handle caught the light coming in the window, and cast a faint glow on the sides of two of the four cold medicine boxes. She stared at this arrangement. The elliptical bubble in the Cutty bottle undulated a little. She closed the drawer.

She checked email. All spam: erections, investments, people aching to meet her, and someone in Nigeria who would guarantee big bucks if she helped him out: "the four millions dollars is under lock in an American bank, with needs of a sponser." As for real messages, none. Nobody emailed her anyway. So next was google, maybe doubloons first, and then the search for Emiliano Gamez.

His apartment was in a part of Kailua she had always thought was "dangerous." She parked the moped on the street because the building didn't seem to have parking, or if it did it was on the other side from the doors. The approach to his unit—116—went along a dirty hollow-tile wall, past apartment doors that were delaminating, so that they rippled. Emilio's door was open, leaving only an aluminum screen door that was so corroded and oxidized that it was coming apart.

She heard water running, like a garden hose. "Yoo-hoo," she called.

Nothing. She cupped her hand across her forehead and scanned the interior. There were piles of mail on the floor against the wall, and piles of clothes, and too much furniture. There was a large wall shelf crammed with figurines, horses and dogs and cats and other animals, and a few framed photos. Through a hall on the left the light changed, or there was a brief glitter of something—water. Then the water went off, and he came inside and down the hall, saw her and stopped.

"Oh, sorry," he said, coming to the door. He pushed it open carefully, the strips of curlicue metal moving away from their proper placement because of sheared rivets.

"This door may have to retire," she said.

"Yeah, it's toast. Come in."

"Well, I looked stuff up," she said, looking around for a place to sit. There wasn't any.

"Oh," he said. "Wait. I'm sorry. I should have—"

"So what were you watering?"

"My mother's orchids," he said. "C'mere, I'll show you." She followed him through the little kitchen, not the hopeless mess the rest of the place was, and then out a back door. She walked down one step into a humid, dripping lanai area crowded with orchids, many of them in full bloom, the colors bright, the dappled sunlight coming past the leaves and hitting the concrete, making it steam slightly. They were on shelves, on the concrete floor, in the deep sink, and hanging from rusty pipes, so that the lanai was closed in by walls of them.

"My god," she said. "This is amazing."

"Yeah," he said from the doorway. There wasn't really enough room for two people out there.

"This *Paphiopedilum* is neat," she said. The flower was exotic to the point of Disneyesque absurdity, with three striped petals surrounding a drooping purple cup, suspended on a neck thinner than a chopstick.

"So how do you know all the, uh, Latin stuff?"

"You mean why, right? I just like plants, orchids. I like native plants and things like that, and have some books, you know, about endemic and indigenous plants and invasives and stuff." She felt herself beginning to sweat. "If I stay out here I'll lose five pounds," she said. She went back in.

"Uh, I'm gonna grab one of these and give it to my mother's friend. Three doors down. That's Millie Leong. She's a Hawaiian-Chinese lady whose husband was a cop. Her kids are all on the mainland."

"Okay, I can wait."

"Actually, why don't you just come meet her? She's a nice old lady, lives alone, so I take one of these to her like once every couple weeks, and take the old ones back." He studied the orchids, and then selected a white one with about twenty flowers on it. He held it up, then looked at her. "Just take a minute."

"Okay."

She followed as he carried the orchid out to the walk fronting the other apartments. He got to the third door and knocked, waited. Then it opened slightly, and then all the way. "Ohh, Em, 'ass so pretty."

Em turned to Terry and moved his head, and she went to the door. "This is Terry—" he said to the old lady, and then he frowned.

"Almeida," she said.

The lady smiled widely at her, walked back to an easy chair with browned stuffing blooming out of the arms, put the orchid on a saucer on a little table next to it and sat down. She must have been in her seventies, her skin quite dark, her hair white with a yellowish tinge to it, drawn back in a pony tail. She looked up at Terry, and then at Em. "So how you doeen?" she asked.

"Uh, pretty good I guess," he said.

It was hot in the apartment. "Aren't you hot?" Terry asked.

"Yeah, but is okay," she said.

"So I'll come back and take this when it's done, and then bring you another," Em said. "And call if you need anything, okay?"

"Okay," she said. "Was nice to meet you," she said to Terry. They walked back to Em's apartment. It was hot there, too.

"So, you looked stuff up?" Em asked.

"I don't think heat is good for old people," she said. "But I guess it cools down at night." She pulled the sheet out and looked at it. "Here's what I found. This is a question sheet I did." She handed it to him. "Emiliano Gamez I found one reference to, but in Spanish, with another name like Anton or something ahead of it. Doubloons are confusing–it's the escudo thing, and you have to look around for values. I have to do it again."

"Maybe it's time for the envelope then," he said. "I have to find that, but–"

The look on his face said he couldn't find it or didn't want to.

"Well, then we should look."

"I–" He shrugged. "Look, this is stupid, but I don't like going in her room."

She looked around. There was a moldy, tired quality about the whole place, and she wondered how anyone could live here. "Look," she said, "you can't be like, 'on,' when your house is a mess."

"'On'?" he asked.

"It's like a clean house is a starting line, okay? Your body—" She waved her hands around. She had to stop that. "I mean, you have to feel good about how you start, and where you—" She shook her head. "Do you have garbage bags?"

"Yeah," he said.

"Start here," she said, pointing at the piles of junk mail.

"But it isn't here," he said. "It's there," and he pointed at the door to what was probably his mother's room.

"We'll get to that. You need to start here."

But he was looking at the door. She shrugged and went to it, looked at him to confirm that it was all right, and opened it slowly. It was dark inside, smelling of mold, a hint of old perfume, and maybe something else, the faint odor of a sick room. He stepped past her and turned on a dull ceiling light. There was a square of dust and clutter framed by a low metal bed frame. She stepped in. No space anywhere—boxes, clothes, odd knickknacks. She looked at the crammed closet. Then she felt funny *something's here* the room contained a strange, whispering silence—leftover electrical charges, muted chatter, or weird static, as if anything she touched would buzz, or shock her faintly. "We'll get to this," she said. Just as she turned to leave the room, something caught her eye: a silver chain with a small, finely carved bone fishhook hanging on it. "Look at this," she said. It appeared to be bound by human hair, or maybe by very fine sennit cord. He looked, and took it off the picture hook it hung from.

"Got a couple of these left. My sister took most of them. They belonged to Emiliano Gamez–I mean, he collected this stuff."

"It's beautiful," she said. It was the color, like cream, or maybe cream with a hint of caramel mixed in.

"Here," he said. "Wear it. It'll help you get in the mood for this." He handed it to her.

"It's okay?" she asked. "I mean for me to wear this?"

He nodded, looking at it, and she held it up to the light *wear it* and then undid the clip so that she could put it on.

Billy had carried the thumb drive on his key chain for two days waiting to load the porn picture on the little slut's computer. To think of her as a "little slut" was, he knew, kind of offensive, but he imagined it would be a term of endearment when they got together, if that could ever happen. In his fantasies at least, she loved being called his little slut.

His chance came when Derek had to go to the Satellite City Hall to process some vehicle papers to sell the old Lexus in front–stupid, Billy thought, because it wasn't worth shit. But Derek had said, "Cruise here little while 'kay? Be back in half an hour garans."

An hour before that, Terry had come in and walked past them as they worked on the Harley. She was on her lunch break and had to go back. The professional look of her clothes was capped off by a cool bone hook necklace, a knock-off probably, although it looked real.

"What, you goin' cultural on us?" he had asked.

She said nothing, just had this sneaky, secretive look on her face.

She'd met some guy, that was it. The guy had given her the necklace. Maybe she was somebody else's little slut. She had gone into her room and come back out, of course locking the door behind her, and without the hook.

So when Derek was gone five minutes, he went and checked her door. The cheesy lock was no problem—he got a thin screwdriver from the rusty toolbox on the floor. All he had to do was slide the blade in and wedge it against the bolt and twist and lever slightly one way, then twist and lever the opposite way, three, four, five times, moving the bolt back an eighth of an inch at a time, and bingo, it opened. He put the screwdriver back and checked the front—no one there. Even if she did come back, he'd be able to close things up because he'd hear the moped a long way off.

He stepped into the room, surprised at how neat it was, and how un-girly, although the smell of girl was in there. There were books, a lot of them, the bed was made, there were a couple of plants in the window-light. He turned to the computer and switched it on, waited, opening a drawer—cold medicine, that screwdriver, a bottle of Cutty, pens and pencils. Memo pads, plastic boxes. More of that stuff in the second drawer. He pulled out a plastic memo pad and opened it. Nothing. On the cover was written, "Silent whisper of sweet flowers in the floral garden—could you show me the way to the sweet flake land—there are a lot of sweet color flowers in the basket." Sweet flake land? Jesus.

He looked out the window by her bed. The corner of the yard was overgrown with dusty brush, a couple of oxidized beer cans in the grass, a pillow-shaped chunk of dark potting soil sitting on the white remains of a large plastic bag. What a fucking dump.

The screen came on: superimposed on the two Mokulua Islands off Lanikai were the words, "do the dream dance with your body on."

"What the fuck is this?" he whispered.

He reached into his pocket for the thumb drive. Now the idea of installing the picture, a close-up of business district activity, was no good—stupid. There was no point. The room was too clean. Maybe it was all the books, he didn't know, but the whole idea was suddenly stupid. He stared at the odd saying, wondering what was in her head that resulted in her choosing it for her screen. The dream dance?

But then, while he was at it, he might just check a few things. He launched Explorer, and then hit the history icon, wondering if she'd looked up any porn. What? A Johnny Wadd photo gallery? Nope. What he got from the past week were coin values, doubloons, a series of coin value websites, Pacific artifacts, Hawaiian artifacts, and a name: Emiliano Gamez. The only Emiliano he'd ever heard of was a dorky kid he went to high school with, a baseball player. He looked up from the screen. There, hanging on the wall, was that bone hook. He squinted at it; it looked real. He sat and thought about this. Tried the previous week—hardly anything—science stuff. Botany. The week before? Nothing, no coins or Gamez, or anything. He opened the "my documents" folder. Not much there. Her resume, date modified—old. A paper from class—old. Doc., date modified—there he stopped. Two days ago. He opened it.

Even when she wasn't there he found it easy to walk into the room, and in the living room, when he turned on the TV, he could actually watch it without the various colors bouncing off the shiny junk mail and scattering that clutter of light across the floor that seemed to suck at the picture.

He had not really looked at her until she wore the bone hook. She had put it on, working the chain under thick brown hair, and then rested it on her chest, and it was then that he saw her face above the cream-colored hook resting against the dark blue T-shirt, and he stopped for a second while she said something weird: "Well, you have to learn to manage your little insanities," and he had said, "Uh, yeah, I guess I do," and then he had trouble concentrating because the hook would catch his eye, no matter where they were, even when she was in a darker corner of the room where, when she stood up and looked at an envelope containing free address labels and a request for money, which his mother probably would have sent, engendering even more junk mail from other nature protectors offering free greeting cards and requesting more money, the hook would float there against the dark blue fabric, and he would look at her face.

There was no point, he thought, in cultivating expectations. She was just helping him out, but the whole thing gave him a strange energy.

And when he went into his mother's room, he sniffed and could no longer detect that tinge in the air, only the remnants of talcum powder and maybe a hint of soap. In the shadows, somewhere inside those piles of dusty boxes and bags of clothes and pieces of furniture peeking out from all that stuff, was the old envelope. And it seemed odd to him that the prospect of solving that old family mystery was not equal in importance to this, walking into a room without those ghost-eyes staring at him with pain and surprised reproach that he had not been there during her last moments, that maybe it really was just a mistake, something he should not beat himself up over.

In the room, he went to the little two-drawer nightstand, where two more bone hook necklaces were. He opened the drawer, but they weren't there—she'd put them somewhere else, he figured. He felt to the back of the drawer, and found an old baseball, pulled it out. Underlined by the curved line of red stitches were the words, "To Mom, love Em," a ball he'd autographed after winning a pony league game.

The phone rang, he flinched. Terry? He went out to the living room to answer it, his heart pounding in his chest. It was his sister.

"How about it? You get a dealer to look at it yet?"

"I have to clean it up first."

"Let's see, that means putting stuff in bags, right? This is 'garbage bag' I'm referring to. They're usually dark, rolled up or folded. You can buy them at the store?"

"I have garbage bags."

"But let me guess. They're not full."

"You can't just throw everything—"

"Yes you can, Em. Yes you can. It's like, pick this shit up, and put it in the bag, right? Then call somebody."

"Okay, but as I said, I have to clean the place before I call."

"Ah, that's right. Let's see. To clean the place, you put stuff in bags, then you place these bags on the street, right?"

"This is true."

"Call Nat. She'll help. In fact, I'll call her. You got her number?"

"It's here someplace. But I can't find it."

"Yes you can."

"I may have thrown it out in the garbage."

"No you didn't."

"This is why I have to be careful about what I throw away."

"So we're back at square one."

"How're things in LA?"

"Things are just peachy in LA."

"Oh."

"Don't dodge the issue, Em."

"It's not an issue. It's a process."

Silence. Then, "Can't a dealer look at it while you're involved in this process?"

"I think it should be clean first."

"So clean it."

"I will."

"Good, because next I'll get a lawyer."

"Who'll come here to tell me to get moving, and what I'll say is, 'I'm cleaning this place first.' Then he'll say, 'okay, keep at it.' Then your bill for six thousand dollars comes in the mail."

"It's called a 'move to partition.' The legal thing. I'll do that next. It's fairly routine."

"A move to partition."

"Yup. It's routine."

"Okay. But remember, we owe a lot on this place, so the profit will be small. We should actually hold on to it until we pay, or until I pay more of it off."

"You'll hear from me soon," she said. "Unless you've got another way of dealing with this."

"Well, there is the estimate, and then I pay you the difference, right? We can get Nat to do an estimate."

"The estimate will favor you, not me."

"But you'll see the estimate, so you'll know if it favors anybody."

"True, but we don't have this now. I wonder why."

"Okay, suppose we tinker with that and see."

"Gosh. Suppose we do?"

Once upon a time a group of young people, friends, lived in Waikīkī. It was the mid-1970s. A young man named Ray Duncan and his friend Doug Lindross met two girls, named Natalie and Maile. They were at the beach, just to the left of the Moana Hotel, where the beachboys rented surfboards. For reasons the older Ray Duncan could not recall, he ended up with the girl named Natalie, while his friend Doug ended up with the girl named Maile. Perhaps it was that Natalie was from the mainland and Maile was local and he hadn't at the time known how to bear himself in the presence of a girl who was slightly racially mixed, with a tiny hint of Asian in her eyes. Or it could have been a coin-flip.

Now, the girl he should have lived his life with was dead, and he found that, with her death, he had again begun to revise over and over in his mind the alternate life they would or should have led, and these dreams were so detailed and so full that the image of her rising from the surf with her eyebrows glistening with tiny, jewel-like droplets of water above the line of freckles over the bridge of her nose and that smile enriched by a scar on her upper lip, her smiling up at him that day they came home from the hospital with their new baby, his new baby with her, the soft popping sound when their baby fell asleep at her breast and its mouth slid off the wet nipple, all seemed as precise and lucid as real experience to the point that it was more real than real life, and he was attracted to it so powerfully that he no longer even halted himself or said, give it up, stop dreaming like a teenager. You're pushing sixty.

He had to stop. He feared he was suffering from some obscure mental condition, life-alterneurosis, or what-if mania, but could tell no one. This insanity had to be tolerated because you can't let rich people whose portfolios you manage know that you wished for a life you could have had but for the flip of a coin or some hesitation at the shape of a pair of eyes. You just had to live with it. You had to live with what you couldn't have, especially now that death had removed the last faint hope that it could be, and Natalie had to live with the reality of what she couldn't have, a house on Diamond Head Road, Oceanside. Ten million. Minimum.

Now she had begun wearing a beautiful necklace that had one of those old white fishhooks hanging there, and he had asked her where she'd gotten it and she said Maile had given it to her when she was spending so much time helping her when she needed so much help, poor girl, and the expression of her face when she had said that bothered him, a combination of a flat, oh well that's how it goes, and the smugness of one not dying hanging out with someone who was, that look of, well, she's dying and I'm not. That's her problem. And then she was on the phone holding that hook with one hand and saying, "Let it go to bid. Make them sweat. Get it up over nine hundred."

Almost a million dollars for a single-wall tract house. Theirs would have still been in Keolu Hills, Maile tending her plants.

"That's beautiful," he said when she hung up the phone, pointing to the bone hook. "That belongs in a museum."

She held it away from her chest and looked down at it. "Maile said it's probably two hundred years old, maybe more. Her ancestor, some guy, collected them, along with other stuff."

"Which is what the pictures are about?"

"Which is exactly what the pictures are about," she said.

"That looks like human hair," he said. "Does that bother you?"

"Gimme a break, Ray," she said.

Billy's boss changed his apartment every two to three months, and now he lived in a mid-sized high rise in Waikīkī, on a street half a block from the beach. Larry Pinchot. Pin Show, not Pinch It. The guy was an importer-exporter and had pimped-out cars and cool apartments. He looked like a teacher or an accountant, but dressed kind of flashy, and wore a gold earring in his right ear, the lobe red all the time. But he was in over his head, rich as he was. He changed his apartments because he was paranoid. Billy had called him, and told him he had something to show him. He'd made the mistake of calling it "dis kine possibility," and Pinchot had said, "One, I told you to call only if you had something important, so this had better be important. Two, please leave your pidgin at home. Use it with your middle school friends."

"Yes sir," he'd said.

Larry Pinchot was a high-maka snob, but Billy put up with it because he was rich, and Billy was moving in that direction, learning a lot. Larry was basically good to him, and seemed to have considered him worthy of his teaching. The first thing you must learn, he'd said, is that the violence you dream of committing under the glorified circumstances of your imagination, is for children. He talked like that. He would absentmindedly turn the earring, then continue: I hired you because you looked capable of it, lethal even, but in this business the use of violence is proof of your failure as a businessman. The tricky part was his business—he imported antiques and classy house decorations from Thailand and Cambodia and places like that, and also slid in things like large quantities of pseudoephedrine, that magic chemical, manufactured in the U.S., shipped to the Far East, and then imported to Hawai'i and the West Coast so that the meth labs could function. I provide the material, he had said. What these people do with it is their business. The man who sells the gun is not responsible for a murder committed by the person he sold it to. You don't look at somebody in the Ford family if a drunk runs your kid over with an Explorer. So, once they started talking about the regulation of sales of cold medicines, the going price of the chemical spiked. And think, he said, how valuable this material is—one pound of good crystal meth is worth around thirty-five to forty thousand dollars. Five times the value of gold. Providing this essential ingredient was simply a business. Niche marketing. You determine what your niche is, and then do business; you do not concern yourself with morals. The police and courts do that.

But he moved because one of his deals involving a million dollars paid by a "broker" for him had produced a large quantity of something other than pseudoephedrine, and now he owed that broker big time, and had to hustle to make enough to pay him back. The broker did not care that the arrangements Pinchot had made with an exporter thousands of miles away were a scam on the exporter's part.

Billy found his apartment—1103, and pressed the little brass buzzer. There was faint static in a little grid above it. "Yes?"

"William," he said.

After a pause Pinchot opened the door. "Come in. I hope this is good." He wore sunglasses along with a shiny aloha shirt and Carhartt shorts.

"It's all here," he said, holding up the thumb drive.

"What is that?"

"A thumb drive. Is your computer on?"

"What is a thumb drive?"

How could a man in business not know this? Billy wondered. With an excited buzz, he stepped to a desk on which was an expensive laptop. "It's just a one gig memory," he said.

His presentation was calm, very careful, as he went from one part of the folder to another, the list Terry had made, the list of websites, the tantalizing meanings hovering around words like "image" and "doubloon" and the name *Artocarpus altilis*, which was breadfruit tree, easy enough to figure out. A trail was mentioned, and in Kailua, when people talked about trails, it was either Maunawili or Koʻolaupoko, and Billy suspected that it was Koʻolaupoko, because in the list she mentioned something about elevation.

When he was done, Pinchot pulled his shades up onto his hair, twisted the earring, and rubbed his face, slowly, with both hands.

"You come to me with a story of buried treasure?"

"I don't think it's one—I mean, I don think it's a story. I don't think so."

"And this is how you're going to get it?"

"Get it? I don't understand."

Pinchot shook his head. "What you want—this Escalade. Let me guess. Cream colored with windows tinted so black you can hardly even see out, and those shiny spinners on the wheels? Of course."

"I never said I wanted that," he said, trying to ignore the insult.

"Why don't you just go look for this cave then?"

"Because I'd have to know where this tree is."

"There are trees all over the place, if you haven't noticed yet."

"No, this tree would be planted in an unlikely place. The *Artocarpus* has to be planted. It's a marker, on one of two trails, probably." Wait, he'd forgotten something. "Oh, wait, one more thing—" He brought up a digital photo of Terry's necklace. There, against a pale wall, hung the bone hook. "I took it with my cell phone, so the resolution could be better."

Pinchot stared at it. He moved the earring. When Billy thought he'd seen enough, he went to close it out, but Pinchot held up his hand. He stared.

"This is a fine piece, the best I've ever seen," he said. "If it's real. It looks very old."

"It probably is."

"How many of these are we talking about? And the list includes images? Wooden carvings?"

"Yeah, apparently a lot. That's one thing. The other is the doubloon part. That's another value thing."

"The craftsmanship on this," Pinchot said, "is amazing." He stared. "And how will you find out where this tree is?"

"Her computer. She uses it to think."

"Think?"

"It's like a notebook for her."

"Can you talk to her?"

"She doesn't like me. I hang with her brother."

"Does her brother need money?"

"Everybody would like a little more."

"That is correct, William. Let me play a recording for you. It's very interesting."

A recording? What was the guy up to now? Billy watched as Larry Pinchot went to the leather couch and sat down. He took his shades off his head and put them on the glass table. "Before I play this, I want to mention how people in this business relate. I owe a man eight hundred thousand dollars, as I told you, because of a shipment that failed because of someone's dishonesty over in Thailand. This phone call came earlier today." He fiddled with his cell phone, and handed it to Billy.

"Eh, braddah Larry, whea you stay? My boss like you know he waiteen on you brah. He tell, make dakine onna corner Royal Hawaiian an' Kuhio 'kay? Six tonight. Yoah man stan' dea I fine um." That was the end of the message. He handed the phone back to Pinchot and he put it in his pocket.

"Originally, I talked with the boss," he said. "He's reasonably erudite, and tends to convince through subtle implication. Now this is what I get—a moke speaking pidgin. Tell me," and he leaned forward and put his elbows on his knees, "does this mean they plan to do some kind of violence, or is this an implied sort of urging that I either pay it all up or else? Six tonight I want you to give them an envelope. But what do you make of the moke speaking pidgin?"

"I don't know. Maybe the boss was busy. Pidgin doesn't mean violence. It's the way people speak here, that's all."

"Okay, so then when you give him the envelope, don't under any circumstances tell them where I am. I'm paying this debt off as quickly as I can. Tell him that, okay?"

"Okay. I wouldn't worry about the pidgin. Actually, some of the sharpest people I know talk that way."

"You're kidding me, right?"

"It's just a way of talking. I'd be more worried about a guy who uses whatchucall—subtle implication."

"Just the sound of it," Pinchot said. "It seems like a threat, just the sound."

"It's really not. It's just the way people talk here."

"Let me think about what you brought today. It's actually interesting, especially the quality of that hook." He leaned back. "As for the envelope, it's no more than papers for a CD I bought in one of his names. He knows the routine."

Billy nodded. He wasn't sure what a CD was, but he knew it wasn't a compact disc.

When your body's on, and was it ever on now, you float, and the little cautionary voice only giggles, a watery distant little-girl laugh that sounds outdoors, at the beach maybe, that giggle that means mindless fun without any wary, watchful attention to dangers outside doors or in alleyways you have to pass. It must have been because of the vacuum cleaner. He had a way of walking around that square of dust that suggested he didn't want to disturb it, and she had thought it strange and suggested they take down the bed frame, but he simply moved it over a little, so that they could walk across the room rather than on the foot-shined lanes on the cheap tiles around where the bed frame had been, and so she plugged the vacuum in and sucked up that thick carpet of dust, bobby pins and peanut shells rattling and pinging in the tube, drowning out the chatter until the square was gone and the room looked nearly twice its original size *nice* and he had stepped experimentally across that space, looked down at something peeking out from under the stuff cramming the closet and said, "Hey, I think that's his drawings."

It was as if she'd wanted to extend this process, making her wonder if another of her little insanities was the pure joy of cleaning rooms, the whole question of a buried treasure a distant second, because she'd said, "Let's work our way down to that, you know, layer by layer."

He had looked at her, well, not at her because he seemed to look at her chest, not that there was anything spectacular to look at, normal maybe, until she realized that he had locked in on the bone hook, and now, walking because she wanted to walk along the little marsh before the bridge on Hamakua Street and look at the birds, the stilts and herons, she marveled at the lightness of her step. Besides, she didn't know where to safely park the moped at his place. The airy lightness of walking felt right, but she knew that assuming there was anything more hanging in the air between them than the job at hand, cleaning an apartment, was a stretch. She was just *yup* helping out.

When she got to his place, feeling a little uneasy at walking past the electric station and its charged aura, which tickled her cells, the door was again open, and through that blackness to the light beyond the kitchen she saw the brief flash of glittering spray, and heard him talking: "Okay, that's good huh? Here, here's more you little shit."

Hm. Why would you call an orchid plant a "little shit"? She waited. He talked on: "Yeah, you like that huh?" Then apparently he turned because the talk was no longer audible, although he was still talking. She went in *he's okay* and through the kitchen. He saw her.

"Oh, hi," he said. Then he sprayed more, and she saw what it was. There was a bird on the wall above the orchids flapping its wings and ruffling water from its feathers. It was a bulbul. When the bird saw her it flew off.

"So that's the little shit," she said.

"Yeah, bulbuls eat flower buds sometimes. But I don't mind giving them a shower." He came inside.

"So today it's the botanicals," she said.

"Yup," he said. He turned on a lamp by the couch. There was still junk mail there.

"We need to do this first," she said.

"Do what?"

"Make space here," she said, pointing at the coffee table.

"That's okay, we can just—" But the expression on his face changed. He nodded. "I know, you have to do this in layers."

They sat side by side on the couch, and when they had half a garbage bag filled, he stopped and looked at the table.

"Did your mother have trouble with her hearing?" she asked.

"No." He pulled a Subway napkin off the next pile of mail and rubbed the spot of wood where the first pile had been. "Hey, this is nice grain," he said. "It's sort of three-dimensional."

"Because a lot of this mail, like eight pieces, are offers for discount hearing aids."

"Yeah, I guess it's just send it to everybody, huh?" He continued rubbing. "Monkeypod, I think," he said.

"No wonder they cut so many trees."

"I wonder if I've got some of that—what? Endust?"

"I wonder what percentage of people have trouble with their hearing."

She didn't mind that the conversation had no focus or direction. It was talk. Chatter made by the living. It was comfortable and real, and even the little voice that floated with her seemed lost in that musing wonder that produced such statements as "I wonder if I've got Endust."

So she said, "I think we have room for botanicals now."

He stopped rubbing the spot. Room for botanicals? "Oh, yeah, I'll go get them."

What were they doing? They were trying to solve the mystery of a buried treasure. While he was rooting in the closet in the other room, she wondered if other great mysteries were solved in a similar manner. Was it "Gentlemen, we are on the edge of one of the world's great discoveries," or was it, "I wonder if I've got Endust"? She was twenty-three and was supposed to be thinking about guys and sex and clothes, and was falling way short, and he was a guy about her age who was supposed to be planning his next move, sex the motive, but he was lost in a speculation about Endust while she wondered how many people had trouble with their hearing. It was chatter made by the living and it made her comfortable and she liked it.

The botanicals were good. They were pen drawings with color added after the fact, of various plants: beach and mountain naupaka, the Latin names underneath in a faint script: *Scaevola servicea*, and so on.

"Not bad, huh?" he said.

"Yeah." The drawings had little in the way of stuff in the fore and backgrounds, just the suggestion of a high ocean horizon and faint lines indicating distant terrain. There were thirty-six of them. "There are a couple others, but framed, in the closet too, I think."

"Maybe we should look at them," she said.

He went and pawed at stuff in the closet, came out with three in older wooden frames about a foot by a foot and a half. One of them was obvious. "That's your *Artocarpus*," she said. "The Latin is covered by the mat." And then she saw the pattern in those faint lines—horizon, terrain.

"Okay, so—"

"This is the tree he planted." The topography was now clearer in her memory. "This upsweep behind the baby tree is the flank of Olomana and the ocean horizon is high because this was done at some elevation."

"Which means?"

"This is the tree he planted as a marker. The line blocking the ocean horizon is Olomana, I mean its western flank, and this on the left is the marsh and Kalaheo Hillside."

"Jesus," he said.

"If we took this up there, we'd see these lines fall on those rises in the land."

"So that tree up there is the one."

"Yup. Maybe he did this as a second marker, so if let's say the tree died he'd still find it. See, this line hits on the edge of the last rise by Lanikai."

"So now we find the envelope?"

"We'll find it," she said. "But layer by layer."

"Some collectors know of the Gamez legend," he said, somewhat dismissively, though he felt a covetous flush beginning to suffuse his body. He looked at her, thinking, why me, why is she here? He'd wondered when he used her as the agent for the purchase of this house, if there would be complications, considering that little thing they had what? Ten years ago now?

"So how are you liking the house?" she asked, shifting a large purse on her shoulder, looking around at the wooden New Guinea masks studded with shells and pieces of bone, and then out the lanai doors at house roofs down the mountain to the ocean.

"It's quite comfortable," he said. "So much better than town, which became really cloying after a while. But I'll feel a lot better when I get the security system done."

"So you'll come here, what? A third of the year, and stay in Seattle the rest of the time?"

"I'll come here in the winter. Managing the collections in the Seattle house takes some work, and I'll think of this as vacation from it. Very comfortable."

"So shall I continue?"

"Natalie, you have a good head for business. I assume that because you are approaching this in the way that you are—"

"Okay," she said. She put her hands up behind her neck, fiddling.

"What are you doing?" He felt uneasy.

She pulled the two ends of a silver chain out, and then up, pulling a bone fishhook out of her blouse. She placed it on the coffee table. He leaned over, picked it up. It was still warm. "It's very fine," he said. "It may be human bone."

"What is it worth?"

"Hard to say." He put it back on the table.

"Look," she said. "Let's get to the question. If I came into this stuff, could I get help from you marketing it?"

"What is 'this stuff'?"

She looked away. She was considering how much to reveal, he knew, because he knew how avarice worked.

"Okay," she said. She opened her purse and drew out a manila file, and out of the file pulled what appeared to be eight-by-ten photographs. She laid three of these out on the coffee table, leaving a fourth in the file. She did this leaning over in a somewhat suggestive manner, he thought, and it repulsed him a little.

The documents were old, the lists almost impossible in their implications. The carved images, weapons, decorations, were a curator's dream, a once-in-a-lifetime collection. If anyone knew about it, whether collector or dealer or sovereignty freak or people like Natalie for whom avarice was simply a disease, people would end up dead in the contest to take possession. The doubloons were nothing. Just glitter, just junk convertible into cash.

He'd been used to concealing what was going on inside him, and was now casually studying the list. "Interesting," he said. "You know the word 'doubloon' simply means 'double' and there's quite a range of values associated with them, but over three hundred of a certain type would imply to me something in the neighborhood of a million-five, or perhaps more." That was wrong, but it worked for his purposes if she felt the value was that high. If they were Brashers, the value would be astronomical, but they probably weren't. If they were late doubloons, not rare, it would not be anywhere near a million-five.

She considered this. "That's what I was thinking," she said. "My friend told me, or—I was told that these are rare, and one is worth about fifteen thousand."

"So what's next?"

She thought. "Well," she said, "I would need assurances that we'd have a deal of some sort—obviously we can't take this to an escrow office, so I need to know you'd be fair in the division of this stuff."

"I've been in business a long time. Some of what I've done is, shall we say, off to the side of the law, but certainly we can make an arrangement. I assume you know where it is, where this cave is."

She considered what she should say, her distrust transparent. Then she pulled the fourth picture out of the file. "Here are a series of, well, coordinates? That's the word. But something's wrong with the picture." She put it down on the table.

He looked at it. "Yes, something is wrong with this picture."

She laughed. "I can get another, I think. I know who has the document. But it's all connected to a tree." From there she went into a story about a breadfruit tree, and how it was planted as a marker, and she was talking with her friend who was dying, this direct descendant of Gamez, who had speculated most of her life over this mystery, the key to it all, a breadfruit tree. And the person now technically in possession of the document had mentioned, when Natalie and her husband had taken him out to dinner at Buzz's Steakhouse, that he'd gone hiking, and found what he thinks is the tree. Bear in mind that his mother had very recently died, and now he says he's found the tree but can't locate the document. This kid, she said, doesn't hike, he plays baseball, for chrissakes.

There was something going on there. Had he known where this tree was, and had he waited until his mother died before cashing in? He has a sister, too; was she in on it? If that was the case, then he couldn't really be in much of a hurry to collect, because he would have collected by the time they'd taken him to dinner. Not to mention that the kid was not exactly organized. If he really did stumble across this tree, then it would have to be a weird coincidence, especially so shortly after his mother died. This hook, and she pointed at it sitting there on the table, was one of many his mother had, along with other artifacts stuffed in that dreadful little apartment. Of course for many years Natalie had wondered why they had not tried harder to find this hiding place, if they really believed it existed, and she had always wondered why her friend Maile seemed so, well, passive about it, as if she had everything she needed, as if the old story were no more than a pleasant family legend.

In any case, when she was helping her friend, they came across the documents, which she kept hidden somewhere in the apartment. Natalie was helping her with her finances, making sure things were in order with her will, and had looked at the old pages while Maile was in the bathroom. That was when she took the pictures. She hardly knew why. They just sat there, and you know how it is with camera phones and digital cameras—you take the picture and worry about whether or not you need it later, right? Then when the son mentioned that he might have seen the tree, everything sort of fell together. He would probably have to turn the apartment over in order to find the documents, and he was probably not lying when he said he couldn't. At dinner he said that he was having trouble going through her stuff. "We volunteered to help him with that, and he said that it was just something he had to do by himself. Which convinces me that he really can't find the document."

"So this last picture has numbers we can't read."

"As I said, I can get another."

"All right, here's the deal," he said. "Very simple. You take all the doubloons, assuming they're there. I satisfy myself with the likelihood that all the wood sculptures and so on are nothing but mulch. If they're not mulch, I take them. How does that sound?"

"Good to me," she said.

"You couldn't just offer this kid some money if he finds the stuff?"

"No, nobody would go for that. He'd do what anybody would—come to somebody like you to help sell it."

"Why don't you give me this man's name and address? I can go from there. We can at least try."

"His name is Emilio Lindross," she said. "I'll write the address down for you." She fiddled in her purse, wrote, handed him a Safeway register slip with the address on it.

"Emilio?" he said. "Did you say he was descended from this Gamez?"

"Yes, directly."

"And he of course knows the story?"

"Yes, I think so. Although, if he knows it the way his mother did, it's a bit of a fantasy, not worth the trouble, almost."

"For the record, okay? Who do you think is entitled to these objects?"

She smiled. "Whoever finds them first."

"And what of this guy and his 'dreadful apartment'? What of his family?"

"That's their problem."

"Ah, then we're on the same page."

When she had left, he made a list in his mind. One, assume the cave was and is dry. Gamez was a naturalist, and he was not stupid. Two, assume that the artifacts are hardwoods, so that their preservation was more likely. Three, assume that there are artifacts of bone, whales' teeth, shells. Four, if the list is accurate, then the collection is priceless. Five, call Seattle and bring Ken over. He'd have to secure the house, though, and maybe he could arrange to have someone watch it while he was here. He had another employee here already, living in Waikīkī, but didn't think he was fit for this job, although he could help. Six, this all might come to nothing, but what the hell, you can't win unless you're willing to play.

He got up from the white leather couch and went to one of the three glass cases lining the interior wall, placed across from the windows so that their contents would not be bleached by the morning sun. Inside, there was a five-hundred-year-old Chen La incense bowl, the contents of which he would not ordinarily address until later in the day. He took the bowl to the glass table, and there, sitting down on the couch, he took the top off, and with a tiny gold Chinese spoon, removed the powder from the bowl, tapped it on the table, and reaching across, picked up a short straw, and placed one end at the small mound of powder. Then he thought, left? No, right. He placed the straw end inside his nostril and drew in one harsh sniff, felt the burn, then the moisture, then his eyes beginning to run a little, and sat back and looked out at the ocean.

The Gamez legend. Like all legends, there was for it a factual basis, as people who looked for shipwrecks knew. Gamez hid something, everybody in the business knew, especially the dreamers and the bigger thinkers. Wealth in and of itself was a cheap goal. You learned early to go beyond that.

When the first expansive, powerful rush rose in his chest and caused him to draw his breath in as if the sensation were a surprise—and it was, every time—he thought, my god, that woman. Even when they were involved, he knew what motivated her. The way she talked, it always came down to getting something glittery but superficial. Her tastes weren't exactly refined. She could not know that the powerful yearning he felt was a kind of love. These objects belonged to those with this capacity for love that others did not and could not ever understand. The worst were those who put a spiritual claim on them, a selfish motive that did not recognize the beauty of the thing itself.

Human beings were nothing. Every day they were slaughtered by the hundreds or thousands somewhere in the world, and their future was to rot, whether child, adult, or elder. They were born, lived a while, did things with tools, and then they died. But their works endured, the objects that these pitiful, useless blobs of protoplasm made were special, even when their creators were not. A peculiar irony about humans—even the best of them, the greatest, were weak, feared death, were petty and sometimes stupid. But when they died, they left behind objects created out of some grander impulse than greed or fear. Someone needed to be there to protect these objects. Avarice was what the rest were motivated by. But this, this was the justified curatorship of the best of man's works. This was love.

So if they were just pictures Natalie took, why did she have them with her? Where would she be taking them? And Emilio, such a nice kid, assumed that it was all right to mention this tree, and he supposed he assumed it was all right, too, but there was that look she got, so badly concealed while Emilio sawed away at his prime rib, and now it amazed him how much difference there could be in people because while Emilio apologized for ordering a twenty-dollar dish, she very unapologetically filed away in her memory the information: a tree near the Koʻolaupoko Trail.

He would have thought the kid would be running up there to continue the search, but no, he talked more about some flight of stairs he was doing for a lady in Maunawili, as if it were more important than a buried treasure that could make him rich. The envelope? Uh, no, he hadn't found it yet.

So, home in the evening while she was out checking on a house in Lanikai, he had found the box on the closet shelf, of old photos from Waikīkī, sure enough, himself thinner, Lindross looking pale, Natalie and Maile in their bathing suits. He studied Maile, almost a little pudgy one would think, until you saw her in the flesh, an innocent, rounded-off opulence to her body, that strange curly dark hair, those freckles. He held the photo under a stronger light, hoping to see more than the simple image. Once upon a time. A flip of a coin. Eyes.

And Waikīkī in the seventies: could there have been a more perfect place? Half of the days of the week they'd eaten breakfast, the four of them, at the Jolly Roger Café on Kalakaua Avenue, where you could sit outside on the sidewalk and watch the tourists walk by. They went to the old theater there, with its fake palm trees inside and Guido Salmaggi playing the huge organ before the shows, during which you might see the sharp black silhouette of a cockroach crawling over the seat in front of you, and now, that theater had been torn down to make way for what? Some huge building he supposed. But back then the buildings were not as immense, there were more trees, traffic was two-way rather than the one-way mess it was now, and you could actually park right on the street. There were cottages and little apartment complexes on every street just off Kalākaua, some of those cottages separated from the street by tall panax hedges. If he could go back and change just one thing. Just one.

There was nothing he could do but dream, nothing to do but pursue that imagined life until it rendered this one as vague as something casually imagined, until every memory was as vivid as something experienced a day before: the smell of her hair, the palm of his hand sliding over her back, the taste of salt on her lips, the sounds of movement of flesh against flesh. And Lindross, that cheap shit. Left her with two kids for what reason he could never imagine. There was nothing he could do to make anything better.

Well, maybe there was.

She got home from work at six-thirty. The yard was quiet, all the cars in the driveway, front yard, and along the side of the house baking in the early evening heat. The house was quiet, Derek at work and the Harley there on the tarp, the oil spots having spread out under it, some part of its guts exposed, the edge of a gear, shiny teeth in an arc at the opening. Beer cans sat around the fringe, and light from the kitchen window threw a fan of lines, spoke shadows, on the bare floor next to the tarp.

She went into her room and looked at the blank computer screen, the whisper of some odd recollection hovering there next to her ear. Emilio Gamez. Or Emiliano Gamez. Why had that name struck her as familiar? Now she knew it had to do with a book. "Otto von Kotzebue," she whispered. No. Way too early. "Charles Nordhoff?" No. "Ellis." No, that was 1823 or something. The name had always seemed familiar, as if some weird fate-oriented thing were tracking her and everything that was happening was just some videogame played by an alien, she and Emilio and Derek and all the rest only electrical charges on a screen.

Emilio should be home. She took out her cell phone and called him.

"H'lo."

"It's me, Terry."

"Oh, hey, are we going to keep going here with our layers? I mean tonight?"

"It's your great great whatever," she said. "He's in a book somewhere, but I can't remember the book."

Silence. Then, "Uh, okay. So how do you remember the book?"

"I think by remembering what library I was in when I looked at it." It tickled her from off to the side *on the way* but it wouldn't show *no, it's on the way* and she began to get frustrated. "Not that it would be of any use, right? I mean, in a book all you'd be able to get would be—" Wait, it's Emory. "It's Emory something," she said.

"Okay."

"Emory—" Tickling. It was there, right on the edge. Begins with an H. "Begins with an H." Outside she heard a siren, maybe a block and a half away.

"What's that?"

"A siren," she said. Emory H.

The siren died off—brrrrrp. Hyde.

"Hyde," she said. "Some guy who came here, a botanical guy named Emory Hyde, maybe 1860 or something? That's his name."

"So what do we do?"

"I look him up on the internet."

"Now? I thought maybe—"

"Lemme do this first," she said. "It won't come to anything, but I think we should do this with—" She couldn't think of a way to say it.

"Layers."

"That's it," she said. "Layers."

She looked on the internet, Amazon first, no, Abebooks, no, then the state library system. The book was in the Kāneʻohe library, A Sandwich Island Sojourn: Including Varied Observations about its Native Population, Flora and Fauna, and Settlers. Now she remembered. She had read the book, or scanned it looking for stuff on plants, and had come across the information on Gamez there. What help it would be was one question—none, she figured, but she enjoyed making the discovery anyway. She drew out her cell phone.

"We can go after work maybe," she told him. "I have to check library hours."

"I can quit early anytime, as long as I can shower before we go," he said. "Listen, do you want to—" Silence. "Okay, this old family friend called, Ray Duncan, and invited me to dinner. I asked him if I could bring you and he said sure."

"Well, okay."

"I don't know why—" Silence. "I mean he and his wife just took me to Buzz's last week and—"

"I love Buzz's."

"—and this time, I don't know. Maybe he just has that—that, you know—"

"That—"

"Concern, that's it. You know, the guy's mother died blah blah—I should blah blah, you know."

"Yeah."

"So it's the day after tomorrow, like at six-thirty? I can pick you up?"

"Sure."

"If you don't mind." Silence. "Well, my car's a beater, but—Hey, I can show you that job I did in Lanikai before we go to Buzz's."

"That'd work."

"I mean, you said you wanted to see it?"

"That's fine," she said. "Hey, so your family never knew this guy was mentioned in a book?"

"No, I don't think so."

"And I can get off early tomorrow if you want to look at the book. Say two-thirty?"

She gave him the instructions—couldn't miss the house—imagine a mini-junkyard, dusty cars from fence to fence, a real health hazard.

When she shut the phone, she felt exhilarated. She had found something about his family he didn't know existed. It was seven o'clock. So, body on, she'd go get half a spicy Italian sandwich at Subway and come home and wait. For what? For the next day, she guessed it would be *fun* and in the meantime she would memorize Latin names *boring* I know, I know, but it's necessary.

Billy had himself draped over the front fender of the old Lexus, Derek on the other side trying to get the bolt for the fan belt assembly free so they could put the new fan belt on. They were both on their seventh beers and he felt a little groggy. But Derek, shit, the guy could pound a whole case and change a belt without showing any more than red eyes. And Terry was inside the house, hiding in her spiffy room.

Pinchot was lying low, so he had nothing to do. Except hang out and wait until Terry's computer showed him something. And with Pinchot, the money wasn't as good either. Normally he'd slip Billy a hundred here and a couple hundred there, but lately it'd been fifties.

"Get on da oddasai," Derek said.

Billy leaned over and grabbed the wheel, and Derek moved around, producing the belt, whose fresh rubber smell came to Billy in a puff of light breeze.

"'Kay, let um go."

He did, hearing the door behind him. He looked. Terry was behind the screen, a dark silhouette, that bone hook in the middle. Then Derek quickly turned the bolt home, brrt thump, brrt thump, and let out a breath.

"Get um?"

"Yah."

A blue bondo-spotted late-eighties Camry pulled up. Probably the worst bondo job on record. The guy inside waved vaguely, and Terry came out.

Derek rose up from under the hood wiping his hands on a rag. Billy looked at his, filthy. "Eh, me too," he said, and Derek threw the rag his way.

"You sold it?" Terry asked. She was dressed the same, blue T-shirt and jeans, but with the hook, she looked different.

"Yah. Just polish um up—fifteen hundred."

She stopped. "I'll get to grow some grass there?"

"Yah," Derek said. "Go wild." Then he looked at the rotten Camry. "So who's da guy?"

Her eyes rolled up. "Em Lindross—remember him?"

"No," he said.

"The guy who pitched?" Billy said. "Yeah, I remember him. Funny first name?"

"Emilio," she said. Billy felt the little flash of recognition, like a minor electric shock. There, there it is.

"I say hello," Derek said. She rolled her eyes again and the two of them went to the car, Derek's walk one of those you-fuck-wit-my-sistah-I-rip-yoa-face-off walks. Billy followed. At the car they were already doing the eh howzit stuff, and Billy got there to see the guy, and also the back seat of the car, which they couldn't use, he imagined, because it was full of junk, shovels, bags of potting soil, clippers, a weed whacker jammed from the back window down to below the back of the driver's seat.

"Landscaping, yeah," the guy was saying. "Like lawns, trim, that stuff. Plants. Plus a staircase in Maunawili, I mean outdoor kind."

"Billy an' me did dat stuffs da golf course lashear," Derek said.

"For real? You mean right at Olomana?"

"Yah." Derek stood away and looked at the bondo job. "Eh, you look like you need one new car." He slapped the hood so that it bonged, and a small shower of rust flakes fell from the wheel well.

Lindross laughed. "How much for the Lexus?"

"'Ass sold," Derek said. "I'd known? I'da held um fo you." Terry went around and got in.

"Nex' time," the guy said. "Eh, good to meet you."

"Same same," Derek said. "See you."

They left. Billy watched the old clunker go up the street, over a bump so that the junk in the back rose and settled, and around the corner. So, it was Em Lindross.

"No surf," Derek said. "What, pound some more beers?"

"Yeah." Christ, the guy was one septic tank.

What do you do? Wait it out. Find out when she goes hiking with the guy. Follow them? Then what? Terry, his Terry, driving off with this fucka soured things a little bit. The guy actually looked sort of cool, an okay how you doeen local kine guy. Billy was off on the edge of it, looking in. Of course he would check the computer, but the whole thing was beginning to feel like a waste of time.

He was embarrassed but there was nothing he could do. She didn't mind, though. It was just that he didn't have enough time to put the tools inside the apartment, and the car was dirty. When he had gone inside the apartment, he got distracted by that feeling again, and went out to the back and selected a good blooming orchid, yellow this time, to put on the little table next to the bed that wasn't there, and he had gone in to place it there and whispered, "Sorry," and put the orchid on the table so that, standing outside the open door looking into the gloom of that bedroom, he saw the cluster of flowers there, floating in the air, a bright blotch against the darkness. By that time he realized he might be late.

And now the tools clacked and rang, shovelheads and clipper blades banging each other as they drove the bumpy road to Kāneʻohe. He should have gone up the Pali and across rather than going the back way.

"It's because I don't have any place to put it at home," he said. "There's that old van full of stuff, and now the tires are flat and it won't start, so I'm stuck. Sometimes I park a block away."

"How many clients do you have?" she asked.

"You mean customers, right? Maybe twelve? And sometimes special jobs where you get a little more money, like this flight of stairs I'm doing in Maunawili. I also did that big job in Lanikai, a whole front lawn on a slope."

"Do you plant natives?"

Natives? He wasn't sure what she meant. "Which are?"

"Native plants. Naupaka and other indigenous plants."

"Oh," he said, looking ahead at the road. "You know what dust is?" Wait. That wasn't what they were talking about. "Uh, actually it's more like lantana and ground covers and sometimes sod."

"I heard on the radio that it's mostly human skin," she said.

"Yeah, but I don't know why I asked that."

"Actually you do," she said. "We vacuumed your mother's room."

He slowed down. Looked at her. "Okay, I guess it is why I asked it. Stupid, I know, but I think about stuff like that."

"So do I."

The area of the library she led him to had books about Hawaiian history. There, along with newer books on the monarchy and cultural stuff, was an old book with a green cover: *A Sandwich Islands Sojourn* by Emory Hyde.

"Okay," she said. "Now we find–" She flipped through the pages, and he watched her profile, her lips moving as she read the words. He hadn't thought about her in terms of the usual, and he wondered why. She seemed lost inside a brain he didn't think he would ever be able to understand, and maybe she felt the same way about him. He didn't know. There were other far more pressing–

"Got it. Here, I'll read it to you."

"Can't we just like take the book out?"

"I don't have my card."

"How about–" He looked. There were people lined up at the copying machines.

"It's okay, I'll take notes," she said. Then she cleared her throat. "'Thus did we emerge upon a most splendid sight, a vast and geographically varied panorama, myriad in its hues of green and blue,' blah blah blah. Let's jump ahead. They're coming over the Pali, by the way."

He nodded. Myriad? Okay.

"'Later in the day did we chance upon a ranch house of sorts, a thatch-roofed dwelling on a hillside with a few small outbuildings, and we were greeted thereupon by a stout, burly gentleman of a vigorous corporeal mien, who introduced himself as one Emiliano Gamez, a former sailor. He spoke excellent English.'"

"Corporeal?"

"It means, like, physical."

"Why didn't he just say—Never mind, go ahead."

"This is nineteenth-century stuff, where writers would sit there and say, 'hm, physical, but then that won't cut it.' Or rather, 'hm, physical, albeit whereupon that shan't cut it'? They used longer words where shorter words would do, rather than today where they use short words instead of long ones?"

"Okay."

She cleared her throat again. "'—and thus did the amiable gentleman invite us to a brief repast.' This means they were invited to lunch, okay? Anyway, 'The three of us were then quite surprised, nay astonished, to partake of a most excellent meal of chicken, the paste of what he called Kalo, the leaves of which, when cooked, resembled leaf vegetables we were familiar with, and moreover, our hostess was a Chinese woman, Gamez's wife.' Did you know that?"

"Yeah, that's my great great whatever."

"Okay. 'So did we eat, before us a most pleasant view. The man Gamez did then show us objects he had collected over the years, many wooden images, war implements, fishing tools and the like, and by way of explanation, did then tell us a melancholy tale.'"

"That's the stuff in the cave."

"And this hook?" Terry said, holding it away from herself. "Then shall we amiably refer to that which I bear with my hand as a 'fishing tool'? I mean, forthwith and thence hereafter?"

"Yeah."

"'—melancholy tale. When he was a younger man, he took as his wife a native of these islands—'"

"Oops," he said. "I never heard that one."

"'—and she bore him three children.'"

"Oops, hold on," he said. He sat back and looked around, his head suddenly full of strange imagery. Three children, a native of—People were still copying, the green light creeping along the seam of the plastic cover of the machine, back and forth. It was beginning to get dark outside. "So this means," he said. "Uh, but that means—What does this mean?"

"Well, it means—"

"Yeah, I guess it's just strange that we never knew." He sat back, trying to remember if anybody ever mentioned this. He shook his head. "Okay, proceed with the, uh, melancholy tale."

"'The woman was descended from royalty, and taught him of the past practices of the people of the isles, and in time he had collected many of the objects connected with the religious and cultural practices of her people. Sadly, a wave of the influenza swept through the islands and his entire family was taken by it.'"

"Jesus."

"'Gamez was a naturalist whose knowledge of the exotic plants of the isles was highly developed, and he assisted us in the collection of some of them. Before he bade us farewell, I asked him what his eventual intent was regarding the wooden images and tools. His answer was, "I shall leave to the future of this race some evidence of its past." The man was much concerned about the natives of the isles, having observed that, like native populations elsewhere, they were vulnerable to the spread of diseases and their iniquitous effects.' That's it. He goes on to talk about the volcanoes on the Big Island. Wait." She squinted at the page. "There's a note in the back."

She flipped to the back of the book where there were pages of notes in tiny print. "Hm, let's see, number 8: 'This story has a mournful and lamentable postscript: Gamez, we learned later, was murdered, beaten to death by men whose motive remains a cruel mystery, for they apparently tortured the poor man first. What they were after, no one knows, although there was a rumor that Gamez was in possession of specie in considerable sum. Amplifying thus upon the rumor, Gamez in his youth was apparently a sailor before the mast, in the service of a privateer of questionable morals and history, and that the abovementioned specie was taken by Gamez in the port of Honolulu decades earlier. Gamez, having escaped into the mountains, and remaining effectively hidden for decades, may have assumed that the debt had been forgotten or perhaps forgiven by an employer either too old to care or to remember. Gamez's wife and child escaped carrying what little they had. Conceive, then, of a woman unable to speak English making her way through the world with a half-caste child in tow. As of the penning of this tome nothing is known of her whereabouts or the whereabouts of either Gamez's rumored fortune or the many artifacts we had seen with our own eyes. Suffice to say that this strange story shall be recorded without hope or the faintest expectations of any satisfaction.'"

Terry leaned back. "Specie is money," she said. "A privateer is like, one step this side of a pirate."

"What's 'before the mast' mean?" he asked.

"I think it's the front of the ship, or where the common sailors lived."

"Tome is book."

"Yeah."

"So my family has this stuff because my great great Chinese whatever took it with her somehow. I mean, this included poi-pounders. They're heavy."

"Maybe she had help. How old was her child?"

"I don't know." He stared at the tiny print. "So he hid the stuff to preserve it. The motive was honest, then. That thing about 'I leave to the future this evidence of its past.'"

"That's it. That's why he hid it." She lifted the bone hook off her chest and looked at it, thinking. "It wasn't for its money value then." She looked up, past him. "The machine's free. You want to make a copy of this?"

"Yeah, I do."

They looked ready to do their job, he thought. Wesley Cotton, the moody one, had picked Ken up at the airport and driven over from Waikīkī. They seemed a bit awed by the view, and by the various appointments of the house. Because he was reluctant to let anyone in before the security system was installed, not even Wes had been inside before now. He'd used Wes for things like delivering vans loaded with illegally bought Thai artifacts, and in situations where his dangerous if not psychotic appearance was useful. He was missing two fingers from his left hand, and that helped, because he usually left that hand in his pocket, and whenever he drew it out, revealing that pale, claw-like thing, people were a little taken aback. Both were capable of taking orders without questioning why, and without appropriating the information for their own uses. They were smart but limited in their broader intelligence.

"Christ," Ken said, looking out at the water and the two islands. "Mr. Kraft, what'd this place cost?"

"Four and a quarter," he said. "It's a nice addition to the one in Seattle. Smaller, but comfortable."

"Oughtta be, I guess." Then he looked back, his expression changed. Okay, so why are we here?

"I want to show you something," he said. He pulled the photocopies out from a file. Two pages for each, on the first, the long paragraph about the 'ulu, or Hawaiian breadfruit tree, or *Artocarpus altilis*, the second, a black and white photograph of the same, with its large leaves, four or five lobes on each edge of the leaf. Inset in the photo was a picture of the fruit, along with a white cigar shaped "spike" as the description called it.

They studied the photo as instructed, read the paragraph. Ken sneaked a look at Wes, and kept on reading. When they were finished, they both looked up.

"Do you guys ever hike?" he asked.

"Uh, did a few times," Ken said.

"Yeah," Wes said vaguely, his distant gaze shifting to the glass case on the wall.

"Did you note the Ko'olaupoko Trail parking lot when you came down as I instructed?"

"Yeah, we saw it," Ken said. "A couple cars."

"It's supposed to be about ten miles long, winding around those mountain flanks and going east. You'll hike that trail looking for this tree. The tree is not on the trail. It's off, but we don't know if it's above or below the trail. You'll take GPS devices with you and when you find the tree you'll record the location and feed me the information. Then we'll talk more."

"Okay," Ken said.

"We'll start at a thousand extra each, if that seems fair to you. This is of course over and above your salaries."

"Fair," Ken said. "Like a bonus you mean."

"Yes. If this turns out in our favor we'll jack that ten times, all right?"

"Fair to me," Ken said. "Must be big then, huh?"

"Yes. The trail is quite long and rugged in parts. So you may take a number of days to do this. When it's done I've got other things I'll ask you to do. None of them will involve any particular drama, though."

"Drama?" Ken asked. "Oh, you mean like, uh, Wes's specialty."

"Yes. None should involve any difficulties with other people, although I can't promise that." He looked at Wesley. The flat look on his face said, if there's drama, I'm up for it.

He got up from the couch and went to the shelf on the wall behind it, just next to the huge window overlooking the ocean. "I bought these but I don't know how they work." They were still in their factory boxes. He took the boxes across the room and gave them to the two men. "Can you figure out how to use them?"

"No problem," Ken said.

"You guys can start this tomorrow. It's too late today."

They moved toward the door.

"Got your cell phones?"

"Yeah."

He watched them go down the driveway to where they'd parked a black Mustang, Wes's lease probably. They paused by it, talking, and then Ken got in, leaving Wes to stand there, staring first up at the house, then out toward the ocean.

When he went around to get in the driver's side, he pulled his hand out of his pocket for the first time.

He went and sat on the couch. Whenever he thought about it, his mind filled with imagery, dark wooden statues, some with grotesque, leering, toothy faces—you could tell by the craftsmanship if it was a gem or not. And the fact that most of them were destroyed after Kamehameha's death in 1819 increased their rarity. These should be the real things: leiomano with their serrated inset sharks' teeth, war clubs of basalt, spears with barbed points, decorations made of whales' teeth.

A woman he had known back when he thought he needed women was disgusted by the fact that he had so many artifacts, many illegally obtained, set out in locked rooms and in basements and attics, in bedrooms and bathrooms. It was the Seattle house, not much in comparison to what it had become later, a perfectly organized museum, but she told him a Chinese story of a boy who stole a horn from someone in the village, the punchline: but where would he blow it? It was some obvious moral she expected him to appreciate, but she couldn't appreciate his answer, which was, 'Why would he want to?' No, his perfection came in isolation, in his own museum, the silent house of the great products of the human race, and this perfection demanded that he be the safe harbor for all he could acquire, by whatever means necessary.

As for Natalie Duncan, she was merely an irritation—a woman whose needs could be satisfied with a few coins.

It was worst when he felt the fingers throbbing there, as if their ghosts had nerves. It was worst at night. It was worst when he saw anyone, anyone look at him in a way he didn't like and he would have to kill. It was worst when he felt again the stinging, and remembered how Marky sang ya-ya-yakuza, ya-ya-yakuza, and how he felt the sting and heard the huge semis going through Denver on the suspended highway above and Marky was going for a third he said when one of the kids sitting on him started crying saying don't don't don't and Marky said let's cut off the next so he can't flip us off and he relaxed, lying there pinned down by those boys, the sting of a single pebble against the back of his head, the gold paint he had sucked through the washcloth firing in his flesh having stripped the membranes from his lungs and throat surely as a blowtorch sears paint from a wall, him waiting for Marky to place the blade on it and hit the blade with the brick, waiting quietly for the sting of it and then something happened to him and everything went blank in a dreamlike explosion of limbs and the tense jaw and the swift movement and the thrust of it and he understood that he had the knife and Marky was lying on his back gurgling blood and kids were running and he was standing there with the dripping knife and fisting his left hand to keep the stumps from leaking all of his blood out and he leaned over and placed the point on Marky's chest and then pushed in, oh so easy it went, my god like going into butter, not even a sound except for the little pock of the point breaking through the shirt, and Marky was still, so he walked away moaning with the roar of the traffic above and burping bile and moaning with the roar and he wasn't able to drop the knife fused as his right hand was to it and when he came to, moaning, he peeled his fingers off the knife with his teeth and walked a mile under the highway to the clinic and said it was a big piece of glass did it and they said what is paint doing in the corners of your mouth and they wanted a police report and he bolted after they had the stumps sutured up and bandaged and he went out into the night moaning and saying, you will do before they do and that is how you will be. You will move on them first before you ever let them move on you and nobody will look at you funny and live. There will never be knives hit by bricks again. You will keep the rest of them. And nobody will look at you and flinch, oh look at his hand, and live. And in the night you feel them throbbing.

And with that itching pair of stumps was the clarifying picture of all of it—first would be his father back in that trailer outside Arvada where he would walk in and explain that you who whipped me with the section of barbed wire, you who punched me, you who said you'd feed me dogshit if you could, you are to die tonight do you have anything else you would like to say because you aren't doing nothing to me now, I am doing to you and it'll hurt but that's the plan what do you have to say? Like to do any praying now or is anybody gonna listen? But there wasn't any trailer back in Arvada, it was gone, and so he left, what else was there to do? Joe Seager said ain't seen the old boy, you his boy? Yessir I am, been in Denver awhile was just looking to hook up with him again but well—

So it was north to cooler country, and way up in Seattle he saw the ad in the paper that said security for an estate. He called, went. Well, yes, I've done this before, and the man put a bowl down that he was listing in a notebook he had open on a desk and said, it's simple, you hang around when I say, do what I say, I pay you ten an hour. And his eyes flicked then to the hand in a fist without the fingers and you said in your head one more time and you're dead, but the man did not look again. Hired him instead, and it was easy work until Mr.

Kraft got the idea he wanted a painting in Phoenix owned illegally by a man he knew and set up a simple break and take except that there was trouble with the information and when Wes went inside to get it the man was there, hey, what are you doing here? And tried to get 911 but missed the last number because he was out on the floor. And when he was handing the painting over, and who the fuck would ever want to look at that? he wondered, Mr. Kraft asked if it all went well and Wes said well no, he was there, still is I believe, flat on his back. But hey, it wasn't that bad, he'll live.

You'd of thought somebody stopped his heart the look he got, and that was okay until he said why the hell did you have to do that to him and inside was the warning *don't look at me like that* and Kraft got another look, okay, okay, just don't do that again, and he knew the look Kraft had because Kraft knew the wrong one would mean the worst for him.

He figured out how to live: his own voice was there in his head, firm and quiet, talking to him—you keep a gun somewhere if it gets to that, if bad colors cover stuff up, keep the gun to put in your mouth if you have to, and then you almost forgot you had the gun because inside you knew you had it somewhere and had the means to take care of everything if the colors got bad and you had to, if it got bad enough to make it so you had to put the gun in your mouth. It was a way almost of showing yourself you never had to because it was there and you could forget it and everything stayed cool and straight. And then you knew you didn't even need the gun because guns were everywhere and you could get one if you had to.

Kraft got to trust him enough that he showed him the inside of the house, took him through rooms full of valuables.

He told him how the human meant little to nothing, but his works—look at these bowls, these masks, these paintings, and here, these valuable stamps, and in this room, my god, the craftsmanship of this stuff—those who made them were nothing but flesh, stinking human flesh, but what they were capable of? Here's a whole room devoted to Louis Comfort Tiffany, who made this lamp, this goblet, these beautiful bowls, using a formula for gold glass that has not been duplicated since. There's two million dollars worth of stuff in this room, he said. And he's just one man. Limitless creativity, great beauty, a priceless legacy of invention. I have this house and soon I'll have another one in Honolulu, which you shall get to see. You'll be set up there in a good apartment and you'll work for me there, part of the year. I pay you to protect these objects, but you might learn from them in the process, too, Wes, because you yourself know what being flesh means—you are mortal, we all die, we all rot, but this—

By then he could look at things dead straight, because in his face, he knew, was his message to the world, thrown at it without even a raised voice: what do you do with a guy who wakes up every morning with the pain of two bruised fingertips on his hand, who looks and sees nothing there but feels it, what do you do with a guy who waits for the look, waits for the shift of the eyes, waits for you to say something you shouldn't, call him a name maybe? Well, you don't fuck with him. You run.

Ray Duncan sat at a table outside the front entrance to Buzz's Steakhouse nursing a Scotch on the rocks. Joggers bounced along past net fishermen on the bridge over the canal, the water underneath bluish and fresh, because the city people had bulldozed an opening in the sand a hundred yards down the canal where ocean water made its way in. They did this periodically, and when they did, fishermen with nets appeared on the bridge, the nets hanging on their shoulders and their still bodies held in their throwing positions, looking down into that water for—what? Mullet, probably. Across the park he could hear kids shrieking, and sweeping above the bluff at the beach were different colored parasails.

He was a half hour early, and on his second Scotch, the clatter of dishes and the voices from inside just pleasant background noise. One of the curiosities of his life, he thought, was how the more he wandered around his house, watched TV, listened to music, checked for leaves floating in the pool, the less he saw any reason for doing any of it, for even being in his house. Nat would call it his midlife crisis, but the word crisis was not appropriate. Crisis implied something that needed response immediately, like say, a natural disaster or a heart attack. No, it was his midlife corrosion, or his midlife meltdown, or—Well, put it this way—a group of tourists came up the walk to the entryway, all wearing bright aloha clothes, making the cluster of four people appear to take up far more room then they actually did—put it this way, when your wife in your alternate life died, that life underwent a crisis, and the question would be, what was left then, to shore up the life you actually lived? That is, if "actual" meant what it meant? He chuckled, his eyes watering.

Is—was. There was the truth of it. She existed and now she didn't. It was strange how shocked he had been when he'd heard she died, even though he knew she was dying, as if a dying person could go through the process of dying for years, or forever.

The tourists came back out, filling the space, the leader saying, "*Conde Nast Traveler*? Put this beach as number one a couple years back."

"Oh really?" a woman said. "I'm not surprised. It's lovely."

They crowded past him and went to the other waiting area. Just then, he saw Em's old Camry turn slowly into the drive. There appeared to be no parking, and the car went by, a belt briefly screeching. Beyond Em's head he saw another, the girl he asked if he could bring. This bothered Ray somewhat, because he wanted mostly to talk with Em.

Then they appeared, walking around the water-filled holes in the dirt parking lot. He squinted, saw the girl wearing jeans and a blue T-shirt and running shoes, and then he saw the white object swaying on her chest, one of those bone fish-hooks. Em saw him and waved, and then they came up the walk to the entrance.

"This is Terry," he said. "This is Ray Duncan, an old friend of the family."

She stuck her hand out and he shook it, and when he got a good look at her, he felt a strange swoon inside, because of her eyes, those brown eyes and that face that signified the older, somewhat more refined or spread-out ethnic mixing, which could have been a combination of any number of races, it didn't matter. It wasn't the much-praised beauty of island women. It was restrained, and didn't proclaim itself instantly. It required a second look.

"—and she's been helping me clean the place up," Em was saying. Ray looked away from the girl because he felt it rude to stare too long, and looked at Em, nodding, thinking, kid, you have a chance. Be careful.

The waitress came out, and they were taken to their table, in the back on the outside lanai on the ocean side. The waitress brought glasses of water and their menus, on shellacked cutting boards, and the two kids began looking at theirs. Then Em laughed. "You know, you've plunked out a fortune buying me dinner these past few weeks. You gotta let me help out this time."

"Nah," he said. "It's okay—got all this money and nothing to use it for, right?"

"Well, we appreciate it," Terry said. "I love Buzz's."

"See? Listen to your girl."

"Uh, actually she—uh—"

"We're just friends," she said. "He just showed me this great job he did on a front yard in Lanikai."

"Sorry." He looked at Em. "Landscaping, you mean?"

"Yeah," Em said.

And he was sorry. He was looking at himself thirty years ago, assuming that their future together was as bright as the sun. Kid, are you stupid? Why is she not your girl?

They ordered drinks, Ray another Scotch, Em a Bud, and Terry a glass of white wine. The more Ray looked at her, the more he swooned with that sense of his having accidentally paved the way for his own loss. He had to keep himself from gawking.

"So," he said. "While we're waiting, I wanted to ask you something. Actually a couple of things."

"Okay," Em said.

"I'm looking at the fishhook there," he said, and pointed. Terry looked down at it. "Is there a reason why Maile would give one of those to Natalie?"

Em didn't seem to know what to say. "Well, maybe. I mean—uh, I don't know. They're supposed to be like—heirlooms?"

"Well, Nat was wearing one the other day."

"Okay, that means that my mother gave her one I guess."

Ray sighed, then laughed. He picked up his glass of water and took a sip, then chewed on an ice cube. "It may not," he said. "Look, I don't like talking like this, to tell you the truth. Hate it in fact, but I feel that I had to say something. It's been eating at me, sort of."

The waitress brought their drinks.

When she left, Ray picked up his glass. "Well, cheers," he said, and the kids raised theirs.

"Okay," he said. "I'll try to get to the point. I know Natalie. I am suggesting that your mother may not have given any hook to her. I know what I'm implying, and I guess you should just hear me out, if that's okay." Em raised his shoulders, nodded. "So I'll go on. As I said, I don't want to sound like I'm ratting someone out here, but I think you should know. Nat had a series of digital pictures of an old document—lists of things, the mention of a tree, and so on."

"That's what my—uh, what? Forebear Emiliano Gamez wrote, and then left." He thought then for a moment. "I guess my mother showed them to her? I mean, that's why she'd have the pictures?" He rendered it as a question, as if offering it to Ray without necessarily believing it.

"So here's the question: do you believe in this story about this man hiding valuables in a cave?"

"Uh, well, I guess we always did. I mean, my mother believed it."

"Do you have that document?"

"It's in an envelope somewhere, yeah, but we can't find it."

"We're sort of, you know, arranging things," Terry said. "Sorting junk mail, cleaning up."

"Why can't you find it?"

"I don't know," Em said. "My mother kept it hidden, except—"

"My wife has photographs of it. Does that make you wonder?"

Em thought about this. "Well, I'm sure it's there somewhere."

Ray took a sip of his drink. The waitress came to the table for their orders, Mahi for Terry, Teriyaki steaks for Em and Ray. They lined up at the salad bar, the noise from the kitchen coming to them in clacking dishes and hissing. They got their salads, Terry telling him that if he hadn't yet eaten the seaweed, he had to try it. He hadn't, so he put some on his plate.

While they ate their salads, Ray thought about the document. He cleared his throat. "Seaweed is very good," he said. Terry smiled at him. "I'll get back to this if you don't mind." He cleared his throat again, wiped his mouth. "You're probably aware of how attractive the idea is, right?"

"Attractive?" Em said.

"How old-fashioned, sort of hokey, like a book written by—Well, or a movie with whatsisname in it. Unfortunately I can never remember whatsisname's name."

"I can't either," Terry said, and ate an impressively large chunk of pickled onion.

"Ah, yes. In any case, all it takes is for someone to be fired up by the idea. If you don't mind, I'll tell you a story. Once upon a time—" No, he stopped, thinking that he shouldn't drink so much Scotch. "Put it this way, your father was excited for a while about this idea, but realized also that there are a lot of trees here, and I recall that when he gradually let that myth slide to the back of his mind, I think it was around then that he began to get this flat look about things, as if he'd become somehow disappointed, that his expectations weren't being met."

"You're saying that he left because of that?" Em asked.

"No, not really. I'm saying that it may have come to represent whatever disappointments he was feeling."

Their dishes came, and amid the moving of plates, the clatter of the dishes and tinkling of the silverware, he looked at Terry. Strange, the longer you knew her the more beautiful she became. Like Maile.

"Okay," he said. "What I'm saying is that while you might think people's motives are honest, sometimes they're not. The last time we took you to dinner, you mentioned in passing that you'd gone hiking, and that there was a tree up there off the trail that made you wonder."

"Terry found it," he said. "To me it was just a tree until she called it arti-something."

"*Artocarpus altilis*," she said. "Strange because it was growing in a place no one would ever live, and that tree doesn't propagate itself. It has to be planted, and this one is old."

"She also found a story in an old book about Gamez," Em said. He went on to describe what some traveler named Emory Hyde said about meeting Gamez in eighteen sixty-something, ending with the information that Gamez may have been murdered because of the objects he described to them and that might now be in a cave. The other thing was about his death and how it left his Chinese wife and child to make it on their own in old Hawai'i. "And he said something, like, uh—" He shook his head, tapped his steak knife on the table. "I give, or leave—"

Terry put her hand on his forearm, and he looked down at it.

"It was 'I leave,'" she said. She removed her hand. "'I leave to the future of the race this evidence of its past.' I think that was it."

Em stared at his arm, then looked up. "Yeah, that was it."

They looked down at their plates, addressed them in silence for a few moments. He wondered now if the story could be true—all these years he'd assumed that it was a fantasy, like the Lost Dutchman Mine, and now it began to take on a credibility that made him wonder why these two nice kids weren't at the moment tramping around in the jungle looking for a cave. In fact Em's response to his warning seemed to be a disbelief about Nat's intentions, and this made him slightly anxious, as if he should take them in his car up there right now, whether they liked it or not.

"You know," he said, "the story seems maybe true now."

"I was thinking that too," Em said.

"Are you going to look for it? I mean, I think you should, what with this new development."

"When we find the envelope," he said. "The place was a mess, you know, stuff all over, and my mother was looking at it—old stuff—even stuff like from when I was little, school things." He looked at his hands. "Even if we did, I have this project I'm doing in Maunawili. I have to finish that first. Next weekend maybe."

"Did you ever write the information down anywhere else?"

Em thought, holding a dripping piece of steak above his plate. He stopped chewing. "My sister and I—" He thought. "We used to play games, you know, making things up about the buried treasure, and I think we used the actual coordinate numbers, 'seventy nine yards to the north,' but—" He chewed. "But I don't remember them. I would think somebody'd done it, but I don't know if they did."

"Strange."

"Well, it was one of those family myths. We'd heard it for years, my father sitting there talking about it, trying to figure out how you'd find a tree, my mother not worried about it."

"Why didn't she worry about it?"

"Almost like she didn't think we needed anything more than what we had. My dad was more practical—think of what it's worth, all that."

"Well, it's true that your mother was—how do I put it?" He took a sip of his drink. He had to be careful. "She was sort of instinctively happy. I don't know if that's how to put it, but I think your father just couldn't, well, relax."

"Yeah," Em said. "That I remember."

"And it could be that she only half believed the story."

"Well," Em said, "it's really only half believable."

He pulled the weeds, looked up through the lenses at Ray sitting there with his newspaper. He lifted the glasses with his finger and saw the fuzzy arrangement of greens and tans and some blue there from water. Nothing else. Just color, dream color. He let the glasses down and everything was lucid and sharp. Glasses bought and paid for with a man's life, and with them he went as far away from it all as he could, west, farther and farther until he was here, the last place he figured where they spoke English, to be away from it. The cell phone rang.

He opened it, studied the sharp edges of the tiny buttons and the little pictures on them, and raised it to his ear. "George, get out of the sun for heaven's sake. You'll fry yourself. I can't have you fried like a lobster when there are houses to tend."

"Yes ma'am."

Natalie had given him the cell phone. Just to tell him when to be here, when to be at what house, what to do at the houses, trim the ti plants, mow the lawn, make it look pretty for the open houses. Now he could hear at distance as he could see at distance. She was only fifty feet away but used the cell phone to tell him this. He moved out of the sun toward the fence.

He pulled a thick weed from the strip of garden by the fence. Something deep brown squirmed in the dirt, then flipped up and squirmed more, and he put his hand under it. A blind snake. He held it in his hand, opened it slightly to study the blind snake's head, only a little thicker than its wormlike body. A lizard, actually, according to the books. He put it down by the fence, and it squiggled into the dirt and disappeared.

Never never never. The word echoed. Never. Those boys made him drive the truck and he told them he couldn't see and they forced him to drive anyway, yelling and screaming and drunk on the flatbed, one drunk in the seat next to him, and he drove, aiming at the ashy tan in the middle, the sun setting over the wooded hills behind, and he never saw the man, hit him and kept going because they were all drunk. Score! someone yelled. Tried to tell them at the court that they made him drive. You drove, they said. You killed him. But I couldn't see and they made me. You drove. You killed a man. You are responsible.

Bought and paid for. The "youth facility" as they called it had good food, clean clothes, and when they found out he couldn't see they said the State of New York would make him see. And he saw. Oh the sharpness of it. The rolling hills and the birds, most the birds, lord were they beautiful, and when he was released they said he could go home, and he thought never never never. I will forget that feeling of the steering wheel jerking when the fender hit, forget seeing nothing but the vague strip of tan that was the dirt road. I will go as far as I can in one direction until I find the last place they speak English. Where there are different birds: mejiro, Brazilian cardinal, mynah, waxbill, so tiny those waxbills and so beautiful. Once a cat walked across the lawn with a baby waxbill in its mouth and he shooed the cat away and picked up the bird, the size of a marble it was, a little fuzzy thing with a beak and feet, and he held it in his hand, then opened his hand, and it sat there and then flew from his hand peep peep peep dying out as it went, so beautiful was its flight. He was responsible for the survival of a bird. This was how you made it up. I will devote my life to the protection of my glasses because sight is wealth. Nobody knows that.

Complacency made her sick. If you thought Donald Trump woke up one morning and said, "I guess I've got enough money now," you'd be full of shit. So when she heard that Miss Hapa Beauty of the Seventies was dying, she said to herself, well, that's how the old ball bounces. I suppose I'd better go say hello.

So she went there, after calling of course. The no account loser of a son Em was just leaving, so she could stand outside the door a moment and appreciate just how crummy and awful and cheesy and low-class that dirty, mossy hole-in-the-wall apartment was, and they had bought it. Well, that was what they were willing to accept, or prepared to endure. It was fascinating to her that they had all started out in Waikīkī, more or less equal, had bought their nine hundred-square-foot ugly tract shacks in Keolu Hills at the same time. And then the true nature of their will, drive, smarts, whatever, took over, and their lives parted, one couple moving into the house near the beach, beautiful and just what she'd expected then, but what made her want to puke with embarrassment now, what with the neighbors on each side being a half-blind retired teacher and a military family, while the other couple, finding their true destiny, water seeking its own level, moved into a filthy hole in the wall, the very hole in the wall she stood before just as Em walked off to get into his mother's ugly old car.

She had a revelation standing there staring at the electrical wires and dirty beige hollow-tile wall and dusty louvers, one of course cleared by fingerprints because the fucking latch had corroded and broken, so that you had to open and close it by tipping the glass pane—she had a revelation: they had all started at life's square one, and because of problems with drive, energy, ambition, whatever, one couple had gone down to this, this ugly place, while the other had come up, but the game was not over—next would be the grave for Miss Hapa Beauty of the Seventies, to be sure, enough of a downward move to put her out of the game, while the other would move up one more time—Diamond Head, a house, lawn, massive Hawaiian rock wall with the blue water sloshing against it. That rock wall would have a walkway on the outside of the fence so that all the losers and wannabes could walk along and look in at that house and lawn. And she'd have a yard man with a little more class, too, not the Hulk. Because she would make it so. Because despite all the frustrating doldrums of an embarrassing holding pattern, she would be the only one left to move on, to refuse to accept the mundane and the low-class.

She knocked and went in. What she saw shocked her in its dusty, cluttered, sad decrepitude. She stepped around a pile of junk mail that hid, she was sure, a coffee table, leaned down with her breath held because she didn't want to breathe any of that shit in, and gave Maile a kiss on her hot, pudgy cheek. "I'm so sorry," she said, and looked down at some piece of junk mail requesting a response by a date five months earlier. Bless this mess? Every time she saw a plaque with that written on it in a store she wanted to take out a marsh pen, cross out "bless," and write "fuck" in its place, because it was laziness and lack of drive that made the stupid plaque sell in the first place.

"There's room here," Maile had said, patting a spot on the couch next to her. She'd been looking at old photographs. So Natalie sat down, thinking okay, we'll have to endure this 'let me take a last look' business for a while. They sat and looked at photographs, most of them from their Keolu Hills tract house days, that Maile recalled with such pleasure and sentimental sighing and Natalie recalled with little more than a dismissive revulsion, although she couldn't show that. She ooed and ahhed just as Maile did, from time to time looking at her profile below the kerchief she wore to hide her thinning hair. She was still pretty, one of those women who didn't lose the youthful look, even while she was dying. Natalie might have lost some of her youth, she knew, but it was replaced by a look of classy confidence, her body in top shape. And she had looked back at pictures feeling a quick stab of sympathy for her old friend. But the truth of it was that people got sick because they didn't take care of themselves. That it was Maile's own fault had occurred to her before—anybody who would accept living in these conditions was afflicted by a disease already, way down in the center of their being, and while she was not inclined to tolerate their weaknesses, she felt, sitting there with Maile, like the doctor who couldn't tolerate the cancer patient who couldn't stop smoking.

Maile wanted to show her everything, as if she wanted to have someone around when she looked at these things that one last time. Photos, weird things made by ancient Hawaiians, something she called a "stone sling" and bone fishhooks, most of them done up as necklaces.

Then she wanted to take a break and show Natalie her orchids, and Natalie had to help her up and hold her arm as she shuffled through the kitchen, and there, holding Maile's arm as she walked, Natalie was aware that she was light, had lost much weight, was no more than a shell, and when Maile opened the back door and they stepped onto that lanai, Natalie felt a panic, a strange, hollow sensation, as if those flowers in all their brightness, bright enough to make you squint, were proclaiming death, radiating death at them, and the animated shell she stood next to had already given in to it, had just shrugged and said, I don't have any energy left to even worry about it, and that made Natalie not only more sympathetic to Maile but also more afraid of her, as if she were trying to demonstrate to Natalie that she should just relax and allow it to happen to her, too.

A mosquito landed on Maile's arm while she pointed at one plant and then another, and when Maile felt it she waved it away, and it hovered there. "Let's go back in," Natalie had said. She felt sweat beading on her upper lip, and closed the door wondering about the mosquito that had bitten Maile, if it would bite her too, that tiny proboscis drilling through her skin and depositing one single rotten cell there, planting the ugly seed of her own death.

Again inside, almost blind in the semidarkness, she had gone back to the couch while Maile shuffled to the bathroom, and sitting there waiting for her eyes to adjust after seeing the horrible flowers, rife and sweet with death, she saw the box of bone hook necklaces, six, no, seven of them, and picked one up, felt it, and put it in her shorts pocket. Call it a memento. Maile in her confusion would not miss it, and nobody would wear it, after all.

She had agreed to visit Maile again, because Maile said she so enjoyed looking at stuff with her best friend, that term bothering Natalie because she didn't feel like a "best friend" to someone she had to admit to herself she'd always felt some jealousy about and now some weird sense of redemption that she, Natalie, had taken care of herself and had taken on the business of living with some will and some guts while Maile had allowed herself to fade because of her own lack of will and guts. She had left that day, feeling the slight weight of the hook in her pocket, thinking, fuck them all. Hold on. Keep a firm grip on things. You don't have to be a simpering blob of shit like the rest. You have stuff to do. You are on your way. That was the truth of it, and there was nothing to feel bad about. End of story.

She went back two days later, thinking, well, you need to indulge the woman a bit. She appreciates your presence even if you don't appreciate being sucked into this embarrassing process. One step short of the ghoulish hospice nurse syndrome. Ride it out and have done with it.

But she couldn't talk like that to anyone. Her attitude about it had to remain secret, because the world she lived in was populated by simpering, gutless losers who knew nothing else but the magnetic attraction of complacency.

Like Ray. Boy did he ever turn out to be a case of flabbiness of spirit. She'd mentioned Diamond Head, and he seemed to change color, as if his attachment to the dump they lived in was so ingrained that moving would seem like death. Experimentally she mentioned it a second time and he'd said, "Why would you want to live there?" to which she said, "Why are we living here?" Then he avoided the whole subject.

When she visited Maile the second time, Maile pulled out the old document she'd heard about for so many years, which she kept in an envelope hidden on the back of a picture hung over the bed in her room, and placed the sheets out on the kitchen bar, probably the only place in the awful apartment she could lie them down side by side. So, this was the legendary mystery of her family. Maile rattled on about how it would be Em's problem now, and who knew, maybe it was all a fantasy anyway, and then they talked about other stuff until Maile had to go to the bathroom again and Natalie had sat there looking again and again at that opening to the kitchen thinking, so, those look real, as if there always was a reason to take it seriously.

And so she got up and went to the document, pulled out her cell phone and took a picture of each page, checking each in the screen. Something was wrong with the last of the four, the one with the coordinates and distances on it, so she took it again.

One thing she knew: she was smart, and not easily taken advantage of, so when Hal Kraft had used his dealer's sleazy subterfuge about this opportunity, she had already figured out that showing him all the pages would have been stupid. That final page with the coordinates clearly written was her hole card. Let Hal, that stuffy, elegant ass, get things in motion. The coordinates she would offer later, but only when she knew that he was in it, when she had proof that he, too, would offer something. God, how could she have become involved with him? Now that thing seemed weird, like some strange cartoon, or old movie. Well, that was over ten years ago, and of no consequence now. Back then he wasn't as soft-looking as he was now, and he was a good tennis player.

Bizarre coincidences like these sometimes scared her. It felt for all the world like fate. How could a bad digital photo suddenly become a hole card, and then magically correspond with a loser of a kid stumbling on a tree? And how could the whole thing have remained a mystery all that time, and then reveal itself now, as if it had waited patiently until Maile died to show itself to her son? That is, if the son was not holding back what he knew until she died, which was a possibility. The sister too, could be in on it. There were things going on that no one understood. She thought often of that first visit to Maile and going out to see all that bright, horrible color on that humid and steamy back lanai, and that mosquito that had bitten Maile, and that Natalie had gone back inside before allowing that little flying inoculator of the invisible virus of death, bite her too. No. Her guard had been up. Her guard was always up. If she was going to keep moving forward, it had to be.

And what about the "rightful owner"? What about "fairness"? She could hear a voice like Ray's, arguing about these things, a pleading, simpering voice, almost weeping with reason and concern. What about the poor family? Shouldn't they be considered the rightful owners? Well, fuck them. The rightful owner was the one smart enough to get there first. That was how the old ball bounced.

In the dollar section of Daiei, she scanned the plastic containers, the memo pads and kitchen implements. He had small fishhooks just rattling around in a box. She had decided to find a new box for him, preferably one with a beautifully nonsensical statement which, when read a third or fourth time, would suddenly take on *do the dream dance* its own meaning. She felt a little embarrassed about doing this *don't worry, he'll like it* but wanted to anyway.

There was "Puti Fresh," a box with grapes pictured on the cover, and a statement below them: "Happy fruits is very delicious, I will eat this and become fortunate all together." She would buy this one, but not for him. It would go into her collection, but she felt that the little poem would be hard for him to appreciate. She needed something more—well, more literary.

She found a larger version of the Folca box. Perfect. "If it always has folca, an important thing will not forget." That should work. She wanted to wrap the box and make it a present, so she went around in the dollar section looking for paper. What about tape? She didn't have any at home. She made her way to the regular stationery aisle. Oops—three dollars. Better just give it to him. But then she wasn't sure—when he'd driven around into Lanikai to show her the job he did, she was surprised to find that he'd fashioned a sloping lawn that resembled the topography of the flank of a mountain range, complete with alluvial fans of grass, boulders, retaining walls, shrubbery, and sluices. It was beautiful, the whole thing.

Originally, he'd told her, it was just a sloping lawn, and when she asked him how he had done all of this, he said that first he kind of squinted and imagined the result, then gone and done it with a shovel, some bags of quickcrete, and other tools. He had even rolled some of the boulders from the back yard down to the front to complete the effect. He had his hands on the steering wheel, and she looked at them and saw the bulging muscles, the roping of veins on his forearms. Now that she thought about it, a little box seemed an odd gift.

It was six o'clock. This evening they were going to finish the kitchen, and then continue going through the bags and boxes in the closet in the bedroom. Then they had to address the problem of the old van and the stuff in there, little pieces of furniture, books, letters, all kinds of stuff, he had told her. But the bedroom and the interior of the apartment first. She understood his reluctance to try to deal with his mother's clothes. They did have a sweet, human smell. You had to be careful not to just attack stuff. She could tell how he held his breath, almost, in that room, and she herself felt the presence of soft chatter, as if his mother were there overseeing their project, but Terry felt that she approved, or at least did not disapprove of it. And Terry's little-girl voice—it seemed silenced by the strange aura of the room, as if the bearer of the voice were looking around with her mouth open, or her breath held.

As she neared the electrical station, she saw his Camry parked on the road near the entryway to the units. She looked at the Folca box and giggled, again embarrassed.

He was watching the local news on TV. When he saw her he turned it off and came to the door. "Uh, hi," he said, opening it.

"Hi. I got you this box for your fishhooks."

She handed it to him and he opened it. "Hey, that's a good idea."

"You have to read it."

He squinted at the cover, then scowled. "What is a folca?"

"I don't know, but if—"

"Uh, 'If it always has folca, an important'—" He looked again. "'An important thing will not forget.'"

She explained this hobby. "—so I have a lot of them. My favorite is one I—" She stopped. He didn't look as if he understood, and this bothered her. "It's—Well, it's a box."

"Yeah, thanks. If I had a hooked-up computer I'd email them and volunteer to help them out."

She looked around. The progress they'd made changed the living room so that it looked nearly normal. All it had required was the removal of a cubic yard of junk mail, and some clothes. "You want to hit the bedroom?" she asked.

He didn't seem to understand. Then he said, "Oh yeah, but I worked in the kitchen. Here, lemme show you."

They stepped to the opening and she looked in, feeling stupid now, for having brought the box. He didn't get it. Or didn't appreciate nonsense. But the kitchen looked almost normal. Half of the counter was cleaned off, a pile of recipes and cookbooks now were squared off, there was a pile of cards, what looked like sympathy cards, and there was an orchid under the window.

"This has folca, huh?" he asked.

Then she felt a little better. "It does have folca," she said. "No question."

He looked at the kitchen, thinking. "You know, Ray Duncan was talking about his wife and all that? I can't remember how much I said about the tree that night."

"Well, the Koʻolaupoko Trail is nine miles long. It might not be easy to find a tree even when you know what species you're looking for."

"But then he said even though she had the photos, the numbers were fuzzy to the point that you couldn't read them."

"Which means if she finds the tree, there's nothing she can do. How far did you say the numbers took a person away from the tree?"

"It was a lot of yards. Maybe a hundred fifty or more, that far away." He took a deep breath and let it out. "Ready?"

They went to his mother's bedroom. Inside, he said, actually it was closer to a whisper, "Clothes. I have to do something about that."

"Do you want to donate them?"

"I guess."

That made her think of clothes in thrift shops. How many of them were the clothes of people who had died? Better not to know.

She got the feeling that he was carefully trying to tolerate her care—she folded each article properly so that they resembled store stock, and fit the articles in boxes. Blouses, T-shirts, skirts—a lot of them. The muumuus she told him should stay on the hangers. He watched her fold things until she became a little nervous about it.

"Would you rather we did this faster?" she asked.

"No," he said. "I like it done this way."

I do too.

She stopped. Then she went on folding clothes. He watched, went to the closet to take more off the galvanized pipe, making metallic grating sounds with the hangers against it, making her shudder. These are nice clothes, she thought. Sort of tasteful. "Do you have pictures of your mother?"

"Yeah, right out here. I'll show you."

He turned on a floor lamp that looped over the couch, and pulled a photograph album off a bookshelf against the wall to the kitchen. He opened it carefully, pages having come unglued from the spine so that they began to slide away. "Wait," he said. He worked at trying to hold the book together, and then, holding it open, put it down in her lap.

There was a photograph of her sitting on the fender of a car. She was wearing a tie-dyed shirt. Terry concentrated on her face: hapa, with brown eyes and a full, beautiful face. Her eyes had a hint of Asian in them. "Wow," she said. "She's really pretty."

"Yeah," he said. "Look at the clothes. Real seventies stuff."

Next to that one was one of four people, his mother on the right, another woman on the left, two men with long hair in the middle. "Which is your father—the afro man?"

"Look closely at him."

She did. It was that man. "It's Mr. Duncan," she said. "So the blonde one is your father."

"Yeah." He reached down and turned the loose page, pretending that it was still attached by carefully raising it over. It was a wedding picture, his mother beautiful in a white holoku with a haku lei on, his father wearing a white shirt and a red sash, a typical Hawaiian beach wedding.

"Which beach is this?"

"The east end of Waikīkī."

"This Mr. Duncan," she said. "What he was saying about his wife? The hook and all that? Do you think he's right?"

"I don't know. Actually I don't know Natalie Duncan that well. She's sort of businesslike and—" A car went by on the street with its heavy bass booming out rap so that she could feel her ribs vibrating. The louvers rattled. Dishes in the kitchen clinked. The television went on. One cat talked to another in a scheming voice: "They'll never know."

"That happens," Em said, and touched the remote button, turning it off. In the dying out of the rap there was a swish and thud from his mother's bedroom, which made Em jump a little and then stare at the doorway.

"What was that?"

Terry got up and followed him as he went and looked in the room. He turned the light on. Nothing.

Then Terry saw something on the floor at the head of the bed frame. "There's an envelope on the floor there."

Em went and picked it up. "Well, it's the document." Above his shoulder was a picture. "I get it," he said. "She hid it behind this."

He came back out, turned off the light. He stood there for a second looking into the room, and then took the envelope into the kitchen, where he very carefully pulled four browned sheets of writing from it, and set them out on the counter under a strong fluorescent light.

"So here's the list," he said, pointing at the first one. "It goes on to the end of the second page. Here's the other stuff, and of course the coordinates, which are kind of simple actually."

She looked. The writing was hard to read, a sort of flourishing script. There was *Artocarpus altilis*, and it was almost surely those words, although the paper had browned and the ink had faded.

"So what do we do now?"

"Go for a hike?" he said.

"Okay, I'll do like a list, because you can't just—"

"List?"

"What do we take? How do we measure?"

"Well, that's a problem. He says here," and Em leaned over the document, "'172 yards as per topo.' Which I think means you lay your measuring thing on the ground regardless of the rise and fall."

"So we need like a cord, in, say, a thirty-yard length, that we lay down no matter what the ah, topo, is?"

"Topo means topography I think."

"Okay, so I'll do the cord—clothesline I think, something that doesn't stretch. You can't do it with one of those tape things that are made of steel and whang around."

"Okay."

"And we need a good compass. Not the kind you have on your dashboard. I'll look into that."

"So when do you want to go?"

"The weekend is full," she said. "For me, it's gotta be a day in the week after, maybe like a Wednesday."

"Me too. These stairs I'm doing have waited a long time, so Wednesday is okay. Besides, if anybody else like Natalie or whoever has the coordinates, they don't have the location of the tree, so we're okay there."

It was easy enough to figure out where the guy lived. He was in the phonebook, and Billy had calculated Terry's habits: get home from work, hang in her room working on her computer, he hoped, and then slip out to go to the guy's house, where they would—and he shook his head, thinking, the hell with what they do. After a few days while Derek was out getting car parts, he had slipped in and checked her computer, and after looking first at that insane statement about the dream dance, he'd looked at the file and seen no change. He had also begun to wonder if Derek was getting suspicious about how many times he had stopped by—maybe it was hey, he's got a thing for my sister, but if he does, why doesn't he do something more than just rise up from the Harley and say 'hey babes, how you dooen?' But then Billy was an old friend of Derek's and they still surfed, although kind of half-heartedly. He missed their golf course days, when they sometimes worked hard, sometimes cruised, and of course played golf.

His next opportunity came when she was at work and Derek called him on his cell to say, hang in the house, it'll take forty-five minutes for me to get there. Beer's in the fridge. So Billy had sat in the living room looking at the Harley and considering what he was doing—fucking over his friends, he guessed, but he had to think like Pinchot. When it came to business, you did business. Derek and Terry were in the way and would never understand the principle he was learning to operate by.

He slipped into her room, carefully as always, so as not to leave the smallest hint that he'd been there. He turned on the computer, wondering what kind of a person would put lists in a computer file, when another list came up, a new one:

The heading was "For Wednesday, K. Trail:"

1. A good compass.

2. A thirty-yard (exact) length of cord. No stretch.

Billy looked around the room. Sure enough, there it was on the shelf, coiled up carefully and tied off with a twist tie, next to a bunch of elaborate plastic boxes whose use was a question—they were all empty. So the cord was for distance measurement, the compass for direction.

3. Granola bars. 10.

4. Water. 6 bottles. Maybe Aloha Maid too.

5. Would you need a GPS device?

6. Folca.

What the fuck was that? Billy stared at the word, then at the wall. Folca. Maybe something you buy in an outdoor store? Like at Sports Authority? If not that, maybe Radio Shack? He could just go in and ask, he supposed.

He checked his watch. He'd been in the room ten minutes, and decided that a history check would be the only other thing to do. At the top of the list was "compass" and he opened it to make sure that it was an instructional site. No question—they were going to find the cave on Wednesday, and because this was Friday and the cord was still on the shelf, it meant that it was next Wednesday, and this presented an interesting problem. If they found it, it was theirs. He couldn't just follow them and then walk up and say, "Eh, tanks ah?" and walk into the cave.

Wednesday was less than a week away. "X number of yards true north, which means cave is on downslope." They were off the Ko'olaupoko Trail. He'd been stupid, slow. The first thing he should have done was find the tree. The second would have been the directional stuff. Shit. Now he had to break into

Emilio whatsisname's place and get the information. Would the guy be stupid enough to leave it around? Yes.

Would he write down or memorize the distances? No. But Terry would. She would make a fucking list, that's what she would do. So he had to assume that if he stole the thing, they'd still have the distances. He had to do it without their knowing. Photograph them with his cell.

He heard a familiar car—Derek. He turned off the computer, made sure it was logging off, and slipped out of the room. He went to the fridge and got a beer, opened it, and was just sitting down when Derek came in.

"Eh," he said.

"Ah. Howzit?"

"Da guy coming fo' get da Lex. Plus he wants da o' Bug out dea. We gotta bag da Harley fo' now an' tool dat fuckah up, 'kay?"

"Shoots. How much?"

"He says is one classic. So if da job good, he give us t'ree."

Derek went and got a beer. He came back out. "You on fo' dat? You know Bugs ah?"

"Yeah."

"'Kayden, we do um. Eh, unless you get stuffs fo' do?"

"Nah, cruisin'." He thought a moment. "Except fo' couple days I gotta work. You know, da man."

Derek chugged his beer, and then burped. "So what, he get you make delivery? Someting illegal ah?"

"Sometimes. I never know."

"Well, you watch yoa ass ah?"

"Yeah, I will. Most of what he does is legal."

They went to look at the Bug. It was parked alongside the house, its green roof visible from the kitchen window. After they fiddled with the car for a while, checking wires, checking out the interior, which was cherry, almost, they drank another beer, and Billy got the chance while they were talking about the NBA and idle sports shit. He took a slug and paused. "What's folca?" he asked.

Derek scowled, thinking. "It's that greenish brown dip. You know, da what? Something like pine nuts ground up with olives and oil? Looks like whipped bufo shit."

"Uh, okay."

"It's dat shit you see at da wrong kine parties? You never know what it is, but you put it on chips? You check firs' fo' see if anybody else eating it, and then you do, before you bag."

That didn't help. Whatsisname and Terry weren't going to any party.

He suspected termites in the railroad ties. This was not good. He rose up from Mrs. Ikeda's front walk, the slope such that he would need more gravel for the backfill, and wondered if the old Camry was up to it. First, assume that the ties do not have termites. Be positive. Get your folca in order. The view from Mrs. Ikeda's Maunawili home included the Koʻolau range in all its natural glory, white clouds on top, the lower slopes hiding the hiking trail and the breadfruit tree.

He was supposed to be up there looking for treasure, but he had promised Mrs. Ikeda this flight of steps leading to her front door, and she was so nice—she came out every half hour with Aloha Maid drinks and cone sushi, so much that he would not have to buy lunch, saving about four dollars.

Something was wrong with his mind, his standards. Here he was supposed to be dreaming of riches, but all he could think about was the patch of skin on his left forearm, which still felt warm, a tangible shadow on it like a pleasant rash. It was a while ago now that she had rested her hand there, but the funny sensation hadn't gone away. In fact, he was beginning to wonder if some essential change had taken place on that patch of skin, a change he could see if he just squinted.

Another thing was happening: when he played solitaire in the morning, he found himself avoiding playing for high stakes, like how good is my week going to be? Instead he chose lower-risk stakes, like will there be enough pieces of railroad tie to do the entire walk? Or would he have to figure out a way to fake a railroad tie using expensive wood? Which made him wonder how the hell the man who had advertised them in the paper had them in the first place, considering the lack of railroads on O'ahu. At the very least it made going out into the day a little less foreboding.

He would not pretend that he understood her. Those mysterious facial expressions and weird pauses made him wonder if she were not quite right in the head, but then, he supposed he was not quite right in the head either. In the morning he had stopped at the door and, driven by some irrational impulse, gone out to the back lanai and selected a blooming dendrobium, three spikes and about thirty yellow-green flowers, and had put it in his mother's bedroom, on the little table next to the bed that was no longer there, unless you called a steel frame a bed. And oddly, like the last time he had done it, it made him feel better, allowed him to think about the day, which came down to worrying about termites in four-foot sections of old railroad ties, and that patch of skin on his left forearm, which he lightly touched.

The front door opened. "Hui!" she called. He turned and went up the already cleared path where he was installing the steps.

"Come, try dis," she said. She handed him a paper plate with a cone sushi on it. "Eat um and tell which you like, dis one or da odda one from befo' 'kay?"

He took a bite. The cone burst with a great, vinegary taste, and the rice inside was good. "This one," he said.

"I knew it," she said.

"It's great."

"'Kay," she said. "I get papaya, banana an' one huge mango tree da back yahd. Plus tangerine an' pomelo. What you tink I should put in front?"

He looked around. The front lawn was a little bare. "Well," he said, "what with the beautiful view here—"

"Is, yeah?"

"Sure is. What with that, what about some natives?" Why the hell did he say that? He didn't even know any natives, except maybe naupaka, and that was—

"You mean like Hawai'i plants lahdat?"

"Yeah, maybe a—" He looked around. "I'll tell you what. Let me call a person I know who knows the plants."

He pulled out his cell phone. Was he allowed to do this? Call her at work? He gave it a try. Mrs. Ikeda went inside.

"Plant and Garden Warehouse," she said. "How may I help you?"

"It's me," he said.

"Me," she said. "And your last name?"

"Em."

"You're supposed to say, 'Hello, it's Em.'"

"Yeah, I always forget that."

"It's phone protocol," she said. "If you use a cell, and you calculated how many minutes you spend over a year because of improper phone protocol, you'd realize that you would have saved money." She giggled. "So how—Or, what's up?"

"I have a question. What plants would I use if I wanted to plant natives on somebody's front lawn?"

"You mean with somebody's permission?"

"Uh, yeah."

"Where?"

"Maunawili."

"Does the lawn slope?"

"Yeah."

"Does the somebody have a sprinkler system?"

"Yeah."

Silence. Then a soft, "Hey," followed by more silence. "Hey," she said. "Maunawili is wet. The land slopes. That means good drainage. Perfect."

"Okay."

"ʻŌhiʻa trees. Either three or five."

"Why those numbers?"

"I don't know. Just not four. It's something to do with death or something, I don't know. I forgot. Do you know what they look like?"

"I— I think so. The puffball red flower? Lehua flower?"

"It's dozens of little flowers that make the puffball, these little hair-like things, and there are yellow and like these rarer apricotty or like orange-salmon colored ones, too. It would be perfect."

"Where can I get them?"

"I can order. We have them sometimes."

"Okay, that'd be good."

"When you plant them, can I be around? It's because of how you have to do it."

"Sure."

"You use black cinder and potting soil. Not red cinder—that's for baseball diamonds."

"Okay."

"You make drainage a priority."

"Okay."

"Where are you? I mean, where exactly does she live?"

While he was giving her the address, Mrs. Ikeda came out with another cone sushi. "Well, I gotta get back to this," he said. "Bye."

"Is it okay for me to come up there?"

"Oh, yeah, I think so."

"Okay, see you later."

"Dis I wen freeze las' week 'kay?" Mrs. Ikeda said. "I just zap um microwave. Try um. See if you can tell any difference." Then she saw the first and second risers that he had installed down by the street. "Ho, I try um," she said. While she went down there, he ate the sushi, now feeling way too full to eat even dinner. He turned the water spigot on and waited for the hot water to pump out of the hose onto the driveway, and then took three big gulps from it. He kind of liked the rubbery taste of the water from a hose, especially an old one.

She came back, looking down at the carefully prepared path. "Is perfeck," she said. "So, how you like um?"

"Can hardly tell the difference," he said. "It's like you just made it. I mean, even the slivered carrots are like you just cut them."

"See? Now I tell my skeptic fut of a husband. Tanks ah?"

She went inside. He burped.

She came back out. "You wen' ask about da—what? Natives?"

"'Ōhi'a trees," he said. "This would be perfect for them."

She gasped. "For real? I love lehua blossom. You can do um?"

"Sure."

"What you charge?"

"I don't know."

"'Kay, I tell you dis 'kay? You great wit' plants an' steps, but you one totally babooze businessman."

He flushed. "Well—"

"You cannot stay in business if you nevah know what you charge 'kay?"

"I'll talk to the person I just talked to and let you know."

"'Kay, 'ass bettah. You like one drink?"

"I'm good for now."

"'Kayden, you do da trees, we talk money laters."

"Okay."

It was true, he thought, staring up and the mountains, that he was a shitty businessman. He had no real system. No folca. He shook his head. He had to stop that.

He worked on the ties. The flight of steps was looking really professional. Mrs. Ikeda was right. This part he was good at. Here he had all the folca he needed.

When you hire well, you get what you pay for. Today business was complicated by the presence of Mei, an ordinarily pleasant lady from whom he got the sexual release he wanted about once every week if he was in the mood. But today she was being somewhat petulant, because she expected more from what she called 'our relationship,' her entire presentation accompanied by the vigorous movements of nail filing. He did not want any relationship beyond drinks and their weekly get-togethers, so he mused that perhaps he had not hired well in her case. The arrangement was, he had thought, free of any of those expectations humans had the tendency to cultivate, and now she had, again, brought up this irritating idea about a 'relationship,' which he had explained more than once was not a part of this deal.

But after the phone call came, when Ken let him know that they had found the tree, he thought that Mei's approach to all of this had shifted, the speed of the file decreasing somewhat, and she hinted that the entire problem could be solved if he provided her with a car, either a BMW or a Mercedes Kompressor, a car with a name that would ordinarily put him off and which she seemed to be offering as the best solution to this problem. This development was a simple and doable solution that would give her what she wanted and allow him continued access to that excellent, youthful body. But he had to get rid of her now. He had called Natalie Duncan and she was due in less than an hour.

"Well," he said, "suppose we go over the Pali tomorrow to the show room?"

"So you buying me off then?" she said. The file sped up. He squinted. She was wearing too much lipstick. Well, at thirty-whatever, maybe she was getting a little extreme with the makeup.

"Yes, I'm buying you off. Does that bother you?"

She thought about this. "No," she said. "So am I staying here tonight?"

"No," he said. "Some people are coming. Business."

"So you don't need me any more than sometimes."

"Look, without you where would I be?" She perked up at that. Where would he be? Sixty thousand dollars better off is where he would be. And there wouldn't be that fine dust of fingernails all over his chair, either. But then, sex costs, whether it's normal like in a marriage, which he had managed to avoid all these years, or through an arrangement like this one. But he was doing business, and that little pale body, now encased in a revealing T-shirt and shiny, tight-fitting shorts, she sitting there with her legs crossed so as to discreetly show him what she could, put him off, in fact seemed almost repulsive to him. "I told you a long time ago, this goes to a certain point, after which it doesn't go. Remember? You thought that was all right."

"Well, I'll go then," she said, and tapped the file so that another little rain of dust fell to the floor. She produced a little pout.

"Sorry," he said. "I have business to do here, which helps fund the car we're talking about. What color would you like?"

"Black." She put her nail file away.

"Hey, classy. I can see you in a black car."

She got up, came across the room, leaned over and kissed him on the cheek. "I'll call you tomorrow then."

After she left, he went to the window and watched as she made her way down the stairs toward her Mini Cooper, a car that he had bought her. Just as she was getting in, Natalie Duncan's car came up and parked behind hers so that she had to pull forward to turn around in the tight driveway. For a moment the two cars were beside each other, the driver's sides window to window, then the Mini drove off.

Natalie Duncan came up the steps. She walked in without knocking, laughing and shaking her head.

"Let me guess," she said. "She's your cleaning lady."

"That's right," he said. "She puts all her stuff in the trunk."

She nodded. "I'd think you'd want to have someone you could talk to, you know, someone with a brain."

"I talk to myself."

"So they found the tree," she said. "We need to negotiate."

"Negotiate? We already did."

"No, we need something a little more formal for this, some kind of a binding document."

"So you've secured the information we need."

"I always had it."

"Ah. This is interesting. You don't trust me."

"I don't trust anybody might be the better way to put it. Trust is just a word that banks use."

"So what makes you think this young man isn't already removing things from this cave?"

"He can't find the document, as I said. It's hidden behind a picture in his mother's room. He can't do anything until he finds it."

"How do you know he hasn't already?"

"I don't, really. So we've got to hurry. There's another thing—he works during the day. I figured that they won't do anything until after the weekend, because he seems to work every day, weekends included, and won't go up there when there are a lot of other people around. And it takes a while to get in there."

"Aren't there other people there on weekdays too?"

She thought about this. "There would be," she said. "If it were me, I'd go early in the morning, and be off the trail before anybody showed up."

"Okay, so—"

"We need some kind of contract here. I won't be put in the position to lose out."

"What court would you take this document to? 'Judge, sir, while in the process of taking advantage of a kid—'"

"Who's taking advantage?" she asked. "That stuff belongs to anybody who finds it. Actually, you're about the last person who should point out anything about morals to me." She laughed, amazed at the absurdity of his idea. "You'd burn a village in Cambodia as a diversion so you could steal a stone image out of a shrine. That's what you said, like, what, ten years ago when—"

"I recall that with pleasure," he said. "But we buried that, as you desired, remember?"

"It was just a phase," she said, "but it was necessary for me, and Ray was going to get suspicious." She laughed again. "This little Asian chippy, on the other hand—What, is she a lap-dancer?"

"No, actually she's a college student."

"You're kidding."

"Guess what she's majoring in."

"Business."

He laughed. "Right."

She got her scheming look back. "What about the document?"

"It would be pointless."

"So what protection do I have?"

"Think about that," he said. "In ways, I have the same problem where protection is concerned, right?"

She nodded slowly. "Well, okay, all I have to do is select an authority to go to, tell that authority about your Seattle house with some very interesting pieces in it, many of which were obtained by—"

"There you go, and I've got a couple on you, one of which—"

"But that's over. He wouldn't believe you anyway."

"So, the information on these measurements?"

"Here," she said, patting her purse.

"We obviously have to do this now, considering that the boy may find the document and move first."

"Well, he's enough of a loser that I wouldn't get too anxious about it."

"I've done field work before. It's nothing new. Why don't you shake it all off and show me the document, and we'll go from there."

She fumbled in her purse and pulled out the eight-by-ten sheet with the digital photo on it, and handed it to him. Then she came around the coffee table and sat down next to him.

He felt her presence, the radiation of heat from her body. "You're looking good, you know," he said.

"You are too," she said, rather seductively, he thought. But he felt a slow flash in his body, that familiar surge of excitement, thinking of the significance of the numbers. "But business is business," he said.

She snorted. "I know."

After he wrote the information on the measurements down, he told her he'd call when he had things set up. A hush descended upon him, so that he wanted less and less to have to associate with her or anyone else. That special, weird sigh coming all around him like a welcome, sweet fog. "So I'll call," he said. His own voice sounded strange, as did hers, and when her expression showed either suspicion or concern, or both, he patted her on the shoulder and said don't worry, I need to set things up and I'll call, and she receded as if becoming transparent as he looked at her, and she said, I'll wait half a day and call somebody else then and he told her not to worry, he needed only to set these things up and he'd get back to her within a few hours.

After he had finally convinced her to leave, he floated down the hall to one of the bedrooms, one he didn't use, now furnished only with a chair and desk and floor-to-ceiling shelving, upon which he would place some of the best products of an ancient race, now nearly gone from disease and crime and modern life. Dust, like all other civilizations. The powder and mirror and razor were in the drawer of that desk, moved in here from the living room because this was the room that would house the artifacts. He sat down at the desk. He drew his works out of the drawer and looked at a patch of his own face in the mirror. Haunted, expectant, waiting. If he could have it all—But he couldn't. He could have a cross-section of the best, however. It was all he could expect. The shelves waited.

Billy could see from forty feet that the doors in the units had deadbolt locks, so getting into the dude's apartment wasn't going to be easy. It was hot, too. The other option was to go around back. Because he had on an aloha shirt and long pants—Pinchot wanted his boys to be well dressed at all times—

he used the forward approach. Besides, in this heat people were either in front of their TVs inside or at the beach.

He had a pad and pen in the glove compartment of his car, and took them out. He rummaged in the compartment and found his insurance card and a spring clip from a coffee bag. He clipped the insurance card to his shirt pocket and, carrying the pad and pen, he walked around to the line of doors, and made his way along them to the last apartment. A shitty place, he thought, unless you owned it. He sensed the buzz of electricity from the wires and condensers above the hollow-tile wall. At the end of the line of doors there was a walkway along the side of the building. He went past the apartment door and looked around the corner, just a wall with cans of paint, a shovel, two garbage cans, and a rotted kayak. Empty beer cans, the remnants of a blue tarp that had all but vanished into the blacktop, leaving its rusted grommets. He walked along past these things to the back side, where the heat intensified. The line of back lanais was there, the parking stalls just outside them. The doors to the lanais had locks, too.

Next to him was the wall of the dude's lanai, more hollow tile, this time with oval-shaped openings, flowers on the other side. Okay. He stretched up to see over the edge—yup, sure enough the back door of the apartment was near an open louver, and all he had to do was deal with the screen and open the door. A bank of shelves holding pots, tools, some orchids, and small bags of fertilizer blocked the door from the lanai to the parking stalls. He had to climb the wall.

He looked back along the walkway—nobody. So he took a breath and pulled himself up onto the top of the wall, and then had to jump over orchids to land on the square yard of open lanai, and there, he felt the moist heat coming off the orchids, fifty of them or more.

He went to work on the louver, but discovered that the babooze had not latched the sliding door. He simply walked into the kitchen.

"Jesus," he whispered. That was easy. Easier yet, the papers Terry referred to in making her list were right there, spread out on the counter. This made him suspicious and a little afraid, as if he would walk into the living room and see five cops there, smiling and holding out cuffs, saying, Jesus, that was easy.

He took out his cell phone and carefully photographed the four pages. Then he looked around. A mess. There was a pile of cards on one end of the counter and he looked. They were sympathy cards, a lot of them. Someone died, then. He began to feel uneasy. Who would it have been? He tried to recall the guy's face again—plain, the pitcher, an okay guy in school as far as he could remember. A sort of haole and hapa guy, more haole than anything else.

He moved slowly toward the darker living room. There was enough light that he could see, though, the couch, TV, and on a shelf on the interior living room wall, a photograph of a woman with a browned lei draped over the frame, the colors slightly bleached. A young woman. Pretty. It was probably the guy's mother. That made him more uneasy, and he thought he should get out, but went to a room with an open door and looked in—he saw yellow flowers, an orchid plant sitting on a little table next to—he squinted, next to a steel bed frame. There was something in that room, some energy that made him hold his breath, and he backed away.

There was another room tucked down at the end of a short hall. He opened that door. It was brighter—a bed, surfboard leaning in a corner, a bookshelf with stained baseballs on top, clothes on the floor, a computer. Should he check the computer? No, he had what he needed. He walked back to the cluttered living room thinking, Christ, it's just like my room except for the baseballs.

Whatever was going on in that guy's life wasn't his business. Whatever he and Terry had going wasn't his business either. He left, slid the door in back shut, and climbed over the wall carefully avoiding the flowers. He couldn't think about this guy's life now. He had to go to the library.

He walked around to the front doors of the line of units and an old lady was out washing louvers. She looked at him suspiciously.

He held the insurance card. "Randy, from da watta depahtment," he said. "You still get wattah?"

"Yes I do," she said.

"Thanks," he said, and went to his car.

Terry motored toward Maunawili, the wind whipping her hair around her face. The idea of ʻōhiʻa trees was set off by another problem that had begun to bother her, especially whenever she touched the bone hook now held against her chest by the wind. If the stuff in the cave was put there for—oops. She swerved to avoid a large piece of cardboard that had flipped off a pickup truck two cars ahead. *that was close* When she got to the turnoff, still shaking, she waited for the green arrow, and went into Maunawili. Concentrate.

When she pulled up in front of the house, a big, nice one, she saw Em bent over and hammering a metal stake in against a four-foot length of some large brown beam making a stair step. He took a yellow drill and a screw and put the screw through a hole in the stake into the wood.

"That looks good," she said.

He looked at her blankly, then seemed to wake up. "Oh, hey," he said.

"We can get the trees at the Ko'olau Market. They've got five of them, thirty dollars apiece. About three or four feet tall."

He looked around.

"Maybe there," she said, pointing. "Make like a little raised grove."

A middle-aged Japanese lady came out of the house with a dish. It looked like a cone sushi. Em looked, his expression a little strange, as if he didn't know what cone sushi was. Terry waved to her and she raised her eyebrows in greeting. "Hea, you can try dis. I tink Em so full he explode rice."

"Oh, thank you," Terry said, and took the sushi.

"Uh, this is Terry," Em said, and to Terry, "This is Mrs. Ikeda."

"I please to meet you," Mrs. Ikeda said.

"Nice place you have here," Terry said.

While she ate the sushi, the lady talked. "So if too much sugar you tell me." Terry shook her head and waved her hand no. "So you da plant dakine? Consultant?"

"Yes," she said, swallowing rice. "Wow, this sushi is really good." The lady smiled. "We think 'ōhi'a," Terry went on, "maybe three of them right about," and she stepped out on the lawn and looked around. "Here."

"Yeah. I tink so too."

"Red," Terry said. "I think that's what's available now."

"'Kay," the lady said. "What dis cos'?"

"I'll do an estimate sheet for you."

Em stopped what he was doing, which was hacking with a little pickaxe in the hole behind the beam. He looked at Terry. Estimate.

"Well that's what you do," she said softly.

He thought about this, nodded, and then walked off to a wheelbarrow, pulled up on the handles and rolled it a few feet up the lawn. Gravel. Mrs. Ikeda watched as he shoveled gravel in behind the step, finishing the riser.

When he was done, the sharp scraping of the shovel against the metal preventing further talk, he rose up, smiled, and said, "Break time."

"So you can do um?" the lady said. "Da trees?"

"Sure," Em said.

"'Kayden," she said, and went inside the house.

"The sushi is good," Terry said.

"Yeah, I figured that out after the ninth or tenth. There's a lot of cone sushi in that house."

He sat down on the step. She sat down next to him. "Something's started to make me wonder," she said. "These things—artifacts you'd call them I guess. The story says something about Gamez's wanting to leave 'to the future of the race evidence of its past.'"

"Yeah."

"So what would we do with them?"

"I—" He looked at the mountains. "Well, I don't know."

"Assuming they're there of course. Look, a doubloon is a doubloon. But the other stuff. I don't know."

"Yeah, I know what you mean."

"I mentioned it because it makes me wonder."

He looked at the mountains again. "Well, maybe it makes me wonder too. He didn't seem to feel the stuff belonged to him."

"Anyway, I'll do the estimate. What do you call yourself?"

"I have to call myself something?"

"Yeah, you know, a business title."

"Uh, maybe Em's Lawn Care?"

"This isn't lawn care. It's landscaping. And Em's Lawn Care sounds kind of lame. It has to be like 'Ōhi'a Landscaping and Maintenance."

He stared at her. "But–"

"I'll just put that on top. What will you charge?"

"Twenty an hour, how's that?"

"Okay, how many hours to dig and plant?"

"Two."

"Okay, I'll include the cost of the trees, cinder, potting soil–"

"Got potting soil."

"What did you pay for it?"

"I forgot. Three ninety-nine. Something like that."

"Okay, I'll make it three ninety-nine. I'll bring the estimate tomorrow."

"I'll tell her I can't come Wednesday."

"Why?" She shook her head. "Oh yeah, the hike."

Ray Duncan sat in the living room holding a Scotch on the rocks and watched little waxbills peck at the tassels of seed sticking up from a patch of grass by his wooden fence. What he had come to think of as his "once upon a time" obsession had caused him to drink so much in the evenings that he feared it was affecting his performance at work, and he did not like his performance at work affected. He'd been good at investment counseling for nearly thirty years, and, Natalie having made her way into the real estate business only fifteen years ago, much if not all of what he saw was from his effort. But his alternate life demanded his time and energy, and this was complicated by Natalie's obsession with stuff she had no need for. That she could not act on that obsession was a good thing, he thought, because he feared what she was capable of. He knew her true nature, but he didn't want their friends to know it because they would lose their friends.

One thing concerned him—she was out a lot, and it wasn't tennis. He wondered if she knew something he didn't, or was busy connecting dots in the service of her greed and had worked on finding this fabled tree Em referred to, which would mean that there was an unlikely chance that she could actually get to the fabled cave before he could. He had to remind himself that he loved her, although the word frequently felt hollow and amusing to him, and he didn't want any change in the status quo, for the boys' sake and he supposed for his, too. There was so much in the past, those early days when they spent so much time in bed, later days when they sneaked off while the boys were sleeping to find a place to have sex, all of that. It was gone now, but he recalled it all with a sense of completion of the phases of their lives, yes, we did that, yes we really had a good time, yes, we—And now it was advice for the boys, both on the mainland and both trying to get through college without blowing their brains out partying and chasing girls.

He heard the front door open. Close. Heard her talking on her cell. "—feeling I should be there, too. I mean, I have a right, don't I?"

Then she went toward the master bedroom.

Be there? A right to? Well, it could be some three-million-dollar deal involving another bid war. But maybe not. He took another sip of Scotch, and the slight buzz he felt expanded and then ballooned out a little, into a dreamlike lightness in his body that ushered him into his other life so that now he saw two people out in the gazebo beyond the pool, one himself and the other Maile, perhaps in their mid-thirties, he thought, their kids in school so that they could sit and talk, maybe swim later. But Maile and a pool? Now the gazebo was on a beach, maybe not a gazebo any more but an umbrella of different colors changing at the curved ribs, and he marveled at how she had gained so little weight over the years, him looking at her as she sat and stared at the Mokulua Islands, that high-foreheaded profile still a classic. Was he ever lucky that he overcame the uneasiness about her eyes.

Natalie came out of the bedroom with her court shoes on, and carrying her tennis bag. "If Suzie Ching calls, tell her we're at Maunawili, okay?"

"Okay."

"See ya," she said. Poof. Gone. She could be gone two or three hours. He would sit there and dream.

The Scotch swoon came back, but it felt sour. Diamond Head. For some reason that move up the ladder of success filled him with dread. The big stone house fronting the ocean, so that they could watch sunsets off their back yard, the vast rooms, the elegance. It would be his death, he knew. Not that his death scared him as much as it had when he was forty or so, but he saw the whole enterprise as the last move for him, one he would probably agree to make, so that he would be comfortably settled into this grand expensive house that he would hate, and there he would last a few days and die. And yes, he would accept it, as older people had a tendency to do. Inevitably they were headed in that direction, as all people were. The only way to save himself, he felt, was to make a move in the opposite direction. If he and Maile could go somewhere else, he might save himself.

Could you make your way in the dark? Shit yeah you could. Billy remained thirty to fifty yards above the trail, hiking through the tall, windblown grasses and over black lichen-decorated boulders, the broad panorama of Kāneʻohe, Kailua, and Olomana Mountain below him. Just in case, he had a flashlight. And now the picture he clutched in his hand was beginning to go soggy with sweat. Didn't need it anyway, because the leaves of a breadfruit tree were pretty fricken distinct, like leaves designed by Walt Disney for a cartoon. Each one was Walt's version of a green alien's hand, but a goofy one, the kind of alien that became friends with little kids. Blork, blork. So you keep moving, but watch out for stones and ferns hiding holes and shit like that. Just walk, up, down, up-down. Figure this first: they must have found the tree in the first four or five miles because not that many people made it all the way to the other end at Waimānalo. Only the hard-core granola hikers would do that, like girls in huge hiking boots who wore no deodorant. Then there were those who didn't shave their armpits—they'd climb Olomana on the way back.

As he made his way over ridges and climbed down into and back out of little ravines, he could sometimes see the trail below him, and he did see hikers. When he did, he stopped and watched. "—view. It's marvelous." "Yeah, marvelous would be to get to the goddamned car." "Oh Stu, please, don't ruin this." "Whatever you say." "Oh, what's this flower?" "Looks like Mason's Sore Foot Daisy to me." "Oh Stu—" And then the wind picked up and he couldn't hear.

On one ridge he climbed around a huge boulder, the wind whipping up the bluffs toward the mountain, and stopped to watch a jet trail, a single, faint line, traverse the sky, the jet itself a tiny glint ahead of it. It was heading west, for someplace like Japan, and he drew his eyes down and saw the tree. Shit yeah. No question. It was below him thirty yards or so, and maybe sixty or seventy yards up the bluff from the trail, in a spot where you wouldn't see much of it. It was in a small bowl in the terrain, one that had a little ditch so that it would get water. The tree itself was stunted, its top sheared off by a hundred fifty years of high wind.

He made his way down through grass and over rock to it. So, from here you go 172 yards due north, and he looked. He pulled a small car dash compass out of his pocket and turned it until it indicated north. Hah, down the hill at an angle toward the Marine base, baking there in the sun a few miles away, and then east 77 yards. Piece of cake. He looked around, and then noticed that some of the grass under the tree was stepped down, and there by the trunk just where its roots began he saw a cigarette butt. Someone had been here.

He was about to climb down to the trail and stopped to think. Terry didn't smoke. And the dork probably didn't either. He picked the butt up and sniffed it, no flavors. No filter either. He knew no one who smoked filterless cigarettes. Christ, did Humphrey Bogart come up here? Were there others who knew about this besides Terry and the dork? And the cigarette butt was mostly dry—there had been rain, always was some, which meant that the butt was dropped recently. In fact, there was a thick column of rain off the ocean, heading in on the trades.

He followed the partly flattened grass. Halfway there he saw a wadded up piece of paper on the ground. It, too, had been rained on a little, but not enough to have been here long. He unwadded it and opened it up as well as he could, and looked at a black and white photocopy of a leaf, a breadfruit leaf. On the bottom someone had written 'leaf—large'.

Terry didn't need a picture of a breadfruit leaf. She wouldn't bother to make it if she already knew where the tree was. So someone else was in this game. He looked down the hill. The trail was only twenty or so yards away, and he wondered—should he go on? But then, after all, if it was a whole bunch of people tramping around in the woods why were they there in the first place? To find a bunch of shit in a cave. What was the problem with that?

If it was worth what people thought it was, then there was a problem. Down on the trail, he looked both ways, then up the hill. He eyed from the Marine base to the path and looked again at his compass. He went back up until he could just see the flat top of the tree and checked the compass again. Then he went down to the trail. Estimate—seventy-five yards. He looked again at the ball floating in its liquid, swinging a little. He remembered the document—he was supposed to measure by the lay of the land, regardless of how steep it was. He would not pace it off. He would imagine he was on a golf course. He liked golf, and he could measure by sight because he had done it before, measuring whether to use a seven iron or an eight iron. This baby was a light shot with an eight iron.

He walked north. The first part of it was more sliding down through grass and over stones on his ʻōkole, but he did it, his mind ticking off the distances as he went—that was twelve yards, a chip shot to the green. He came to a shelf, and stopped. That column of rain had swept through Kailua now, and was headed in his direction. It was eating up the Pali Highway, moving as a single dense column, wide enough to blank out the west flank of Olomana Mountain and eating up jungle as it went, coming his way.

So he would get wet while he was counting off distances. The wind picked up. He continued down the bluff, holding the compass out, until he thought he'd made it the ninety-five yards from the trail. Here he was standing on another shelf. Figure this: if a guy wanted to put his stuff in a cave, he'd have to have some recognizable first point to turn himself toward the cave, but of course he started at the cave and went backwards, finding himself on this shelf and then testing whether or not due south was the line to the tree. You had to think like somebody who wanted to set up these locations. He stood by his cave and said, okay, let's go east until it looks right.

He heard the rain now, a roar inside an increasing wind, saw raindrops spattering the leaves of ginger and various other plants, the whole thing coming now as a loud hissing sound, and he saw the plants and trees down the bluff fuzzing out and vanishing in it, and looked around for shelter, which was right there under a small tree, and he made his way to it just as the first large drops pelted leaves on the ground before him.

And then it was coming down all around him, a hissing roar of heavy rain bouncing in tiny diamonds right by his sneakers, heavy drops coming through the leaves of the tree he was under and wetting his head. He waited it out, the sound of it some weird music that shut his brain down so that he crouched there looking down at rocks, little bugs running around in a panic, his compass dancing in the plastic sphere, and the veins of his forearms. He waited until he heard that roar go up the mountain, and when it was over the sun was out again, and he stood up and looked around, shaking water out of his hair.

Every leaf was slick and gleaming, dripping diamonds onto the ground. Little rivulets ran between rocks. Steam came off boulders. He looked once again at the compass and whispered, "What the fuck am I doing?" Tramping around with a compass looking for a cave, trying to prove to a mainland haole drug runner who called him William that he wasn't stupid. Carrying envelopes to people. Taking a pickup truck with a five-gallon can of some toxic shit to some guy on the north shore. And doing a good job too. All to impress a haole criminal and prove that he, William, pordagee and haole and who knew what the hell else, was not a moke.

What, after all, is the use of it? he thought, looking at the bright, dripping leaves. Maybe there was no use. But he was committed. He said he'd do this and he would do it.

The seventy-two yards east were a problem because of the terrain, but as he looked around, he could tell that he was close. That man Mr. Gamez stood by the cave and looked west and said, here's what I'll do—I'll go to that shelf over there and then see if exact south leads me to a place where—sure, all you had to do was think like somebody out to hide something, and you could go backwards from that to the hiding place.

But the cigarette butt bothered him. How could there be anyone else but Terry and the doofus involved in this? Had Pinchot set some other people on this search too? He drew out his cell phone. The sun was going behind the mountain, its shade crawling along the bluff toward him at an angle. He started to scroll through numbers and remembered that Pinchot didn't want his number on anyone's cell phone.

He dialed him from memory. When he answered Billy said, "This is William."

"Yes? And?"

"Did you send anybody else up here to look?"

"No I didn't. Why?"

"I found the tree."

"Good."

"And found a cigarette butt and stomped down grass. And I found a picture of a breadfruit leaf. Somebody else is in this too, I think."

"The girl you mentioned."

"No. She works. The guy works, doesn't smoke."

"What about the cave?"

"I'm close, but it'll get dark soon."

"Well, look as long as you can and then tomorrow."

"Okay."

"If this works out, there's a good cut for you, William. I promise. Come by tomorrow evening. I have something for you to do. Six or so."

"Okay."

"Talk to you later."

So, look a little longer. He put the phone in his pocket and began walking along a steep bank, holding the compass out. When he thought he'd gone the right distance, estimating by the length of shot he'd use with a pitching wedge, he was standing on a steep bank. The wet grass was lying over, little muddy rivulets on the ground. There was no evidence of people stomping around. There was a rock shelf above him, and then farther to the east a place where that shelf dropped at a slight angle in a cluster of brush, vines, and ferns, those light-colored ones he'd been told when he was a kid not to step on when you were hiking, because they sometimes hid holes, lava tubes. Caves.

He saw the problem now—if there was an opening to any cave there, you'd have to have a ladder to get to it unless you were a monkey. Ten feet maybe. Above that the shelf that vanished into the brush and vines was rock, boulders, all at about a thirty- degree angle going up toward the trail. You couldn't approach from above. If the cave was there, it was one boss hiding place.

He walked toward the brush and ferns, checking the compass—yup, right on target—and ended up standing there looking at the ferns and vines, dripping and dull green because the sun had gone over the mountain. He tried pulling himself up the bank to check out the ferns. Once he got high enough to grab a handful of fern, he snaked himself, muddying his shirt and sneakers. He felt through the ferns—rock, more rock, then found a good handhold. He pulled himself along until the handhold angled upward, and found himself staring at fern leaves and feeling cooler air on his fingers. He tried working at the vines to get himself up higher, and heard the rain again. Turning to look, he saw another column of it marching up the highway and up the flanks of the mountain range toward him. Well, shit, get wet then.

He pulled himself sideways so that he now had both hands over the lip of the opening, and with all the strength he had, he hauled himself up and jammed his face into the ferns. First he saw a tree root, like a thick pillar, and next to that an oblong hole with blackness beyond it, so that the opening was like a large frown, the tree root in the middle. He stared into the opening. It was too small, and he figured out why—the top shelf above the cave had collapsed partway, maybe a hundred years ago. He pulled his face closer, and a strange smell, soil, came to him along with the feeling of a hushed echo—he could not tell how far in it went, because of the darkness. He squinted into it. There were points of light because of his own fatigue, there was that echo, that strange hush of stuff placed here by someone from a hundred fifty years ago, stuff the man wanted to save, and here he was finding this after all this time just to prove to a criminal that he wasn't stupid. And whose stuff was this? He had the odd, almost frightening feeling that this was not his shit to mess with, and as if to prove him right, the rain swept up the hill and drenched him where he hung staring into that black hole. He had disturbed something he should not have disturbed. He held himself steady with one hand and tried pulling the ferns back over the opening, to cover it back up. Then he tried to let himself down the bank, but slid and banged his knee on a rock on the way, but ended up standing, looking down at his muddy shirt. He turned and faced the rain, stood there feeling it powerwash the mud off his shirt and sneakers. "Fuck dis," he said. "I not doing dis. Fuck it."

As usual, he turned on his computer and played solitaire. No you don't, he thought. You don't play for tomorrow, or a good life, or money. You are playing a game. He was halfway through the game when the stupid fatal error box came on, and he turned it off. So. Proof enough that playing for a good life was a bad idea. He had to put a stop to it anyway. He went through the kitchen to water the orchids. Stopped. There was a single purple flower on the floor. He stared at it. The one he had put in his mother's room was yellow. How could he step on a purple one? He slid the door open, and looked at the orchids. They were fine, except that on the left, one of them was leaning. He set it up straight and turned to go back in. He picked up the crushed flower and put it in the already full wastebasket. He looked at the counter at the document pages, and then went back out to the orchids. Something wasn't right. He took the hose and began misting the orchids, looking around. The wall on the left side on top where the two-by-four capped it looked different. He leaned up, and saw that some dust was gone. But it was nearly dark. He moved to the wall and touched the top—no dust, no grit.

Somebody had come over that wall, had opened the door he rarely locked, and had gone inside. He finished watering and went inside. Nothing different. He opened the door to his room—surfboard, baseballs, nothing wrong. He went and opened the door to his mother's room, and saw the orchid he had to water and knew someone had looked in there. He pulled out his cell phone.

"Boy did I get drenched going through Kailua," she said.

"Somebody's been in our place. Or, I mean, my apartment."

"Really? How do you know?"

"A flower." He explained it to her, and reminded her that the document was right there for anybody to look at.

"Did they take anything?"

"No, that's the problem. It means that Mr. Duncan was probably right."

"What do you want to do?"

"Well, I think we hafta go up there as soon as we can."

"When?"

"Tomorrow. We had Wednesday, but I think it has to be tomorrow."

"I can call a friend of mine to sub for me tomorrow. There's no reason to wait. We can go early."

"Okay, say, eight?"

"No, I mean early. I think we should be there way before sunrise."

He felt a little stab. Before sunrise? Was she crazy? "Uh, why then?"

"Because if someone else has the information about how to find this cave, they'll get there first. We should go before sunrise."

She was right. "You're right."

"Pick me up at four."

"Uh, four?"

"Yeah, four. I'll be outside."

"It's stupid, but my alarm is set for seven and I don't know how to change it. Maybe—"

"I'll call you," she said.

After he shut his phone he stood in the kitchen thinking. Would his mother's friend do this? It seemed inconceivable, and then he thought he had to be mistaken, that this flower on the floor was one that came in on the bottom of his foot. He felt somewhat ashamed of himself for having suspected it, and recalled the conversation with Mr. Duncan, whose concerns about his wife had seemed strange, if not a little paranoid. No, Natalie Duncan might have been sort of hard, domineering the word might be, but she wouldn't do this.

He made another, more thorough search of the living room, then his room, and found nothing. When he opened his mother's room door, he saw the orchid, went back to the kitchen and got a glass of water, and went into the room to water it, and knew again that someone had been there.

He had always felt that overheard phone calls were overheard only because the snooper did not clear a throat or make a noise or otherwise signal his or her presence to the person on the phone. It was the kind of thing his wife would do. But Ray, this evening, was sitting outside and looking beyond the pool at the gazebo, so immersed in his dream, in complicated revisions and developments of it that, on his sixth Scotch, the presence of the voice made him flinch with the pain and irritation of reality.

What he heard first was "—eight? So who else is coming? People you provide?" Then after a silence: "—should have done this days ago, because the loser might have gone up there already. How can you assume—" and then she turned away. He sat there, the gazebo swimming in his vision, the ghostly shapes of people inside, and "—won't be taken advantage of in this deal. I'm the one who gave you the—" and he sighed, thought, my god, can you believe this? "—got it. Me.

So just remember that okay?" Apparently she hung up there, because he then heard her stomping off to another part of the house. That's what she did when she was agitated. She stomped. Far off now he heard the squeak of her court shoes. She was in the bathroom.

While she was showering, he went inside to get another drink. Why not? At least it dulled the amazement he felt at just how far she was willing to go to get what she wanted. In this case it was a house on Diamond Head because the one they were in and which he liked and had felt was his last home was a dump to her, a low-class shack.

He looked at the paper on the counter and flipped through the real estate section to see just how absurd the prices for houses on Diamond Head had become. There was one for nine million—a possibility, unless she felt that it, too, was a dump. There was one in Kāhala for eight million—no, too cheesy, probably. How about Neverland? She could probably have it for fifty. He didn't like thinking this way. What was wrong with drive, determination and pluck? Well, nothing, he supposed. What was wrong with calculatedly fucking over the son of your best friend? Well, nothing, he supposed. It was business. The rules of engagement were clear—do unto others before they do unto you. And feel no remorse. After all, remorse, along with honesty, sympathy, and all those good things were character features of another century. He even felt that, despite his best efforts, his sons had picked up on this new ethic, too.

He read through the real estate listings, and ended up scanning the Kailua offerings, vaguely thinking of seeing how much houses in his neighborhood cost, and saw a listing for a two bedroom one bath house in Keolu Hills. There was a picture, and it resembled the little house they once lived in. Five fifty-nine. Cheap by current standards.

Natalie came out of the bathroom wearing shorts and an oversized T-shirt with a Roxy logo on the front. She went to the refrigerator and pulled out a half-full bottle of wine and poured herself a glass.

"How was tennis?" he asked.

"Okay."

"Look at this," he said, placing his finger under the picture of the little Keolu Hills house.

She looked.

"Remember?" he asked.

She snorted. "Yeah, I remember."

"I think you and I should buy this house."

"Bad investment," she said. "There's no increase potential in low-end stuff. You know that."

"No, I mean to live in."

She stared at him. "You're drunk," she said. "Or you're crazy."

"It's both, I believe."

"Okay, at least we've got that settled." She looked around as if distracted by something.

"I know," he said. "Business is complicated. Business is demanding and distracting."

"Yes it is," she said. "Let me guess. This is your seventh scotch." She held up her glass. "To my one wine."

"You are correct," he said. "Good call."

"Now, let's figure out why you're baiting me."

"Actually, you already took the bait. It was that hook you lifted from Maile."

"She gave it to me," she said.

"Well, I shall take your word for it. Why did I think you lifted it when she wasn't looking? Strange."

"So this conversation is finished?"

"Well, no, it's not."

"Ah."

"There is that other trivial matter—"

"Yes."

"—of the interesting plan of taking advantage of 'the loser' whom I assume is Em."

"Zia's," she said. "That's where I'd like to eat tonight."

"And whoever you've hooked up with to help you—"

"Linguini in clam sauce. That's my favorite."

"—fuck over the son of your best friend. Seems a little callous even for business, the way I see it."

"Too late for reservations," she said, looking at her watch. "Bummer."

"So—"

"Look, do you want to eat out?"

"No, I want to drink another Scotch."

She stared, then seemed to realize something. "You eavesdropped on my conversation."

"I couldn't help it. I was sitting outside appreciating my back yard, which I like, and heard some of it. I didn't clear my throat or cough. Sorry."

"And now you're all indignant about it. I can tell. 'God how awful. She's trying to get there first. Oh how horrible.'"

"Well, I thought she was your friend."

"Yeah. My one-time best friend. Even she said that. Well, the best friend thing is for junior high, or haven't you figured that out yet?"

"I suppose I should have."

"I suppose."

"It's just that we've known their family for so long. You know, we've been concerned about how they'd been doing, and this last thing—"

"Shit happens."

"—was sad. It—"

"No, it was just a sign, a measure of how we're doing."

"Well, I was going to ask you to maybe drop this, you know, drop the business of trying to take away that kid's chance to—"

"It doesn't belong to him. It belongs to whoever gets there first. Everything belongs to whoever gets there first."

"Isn't it 'whomever'? I never get that right. I should look it up."

"You should. It'll make you feel better."

"I know. It's 'whom' because it comes after what you call a—A preposition? No, it's because it takes some other position?"

"Sounds right. That sounds dead on, Ray."

"And you'd refer to Em as a 'loser'? Would you refer to your own kids that way, too?"

"If they were losers I would. They're not, so I'm keeping my fingers crossed. Should they become losers, I'll begin referring to them as losers."

"Am I a loser?"

She stared at him, thinking. "No, you're just complacent. It's sad, really."

"Okay, I was just wondering."

"Complacency is just a weakness. It's okay really. No 'L' word for you."

"Yet."

"So, now are we finished?"

"So, who is the person helping you with this? I was just wondering."

"Oh Ray, do you really need to know? Does it really matter?"

"No, I suppose it doesn't."

"Good."

"Well, I don't think you should do it. But of course the cat is out of the bag, isn't it?"

"It is. Yes. But please, if you just forget about it and, say, appreciate your yard, you'll feel better. I've got to make another call now."

"Yes. I appreciate my yard. I really do."

It felt sour to him, the whole thing. He drove over the Pali planning to explain to Pinchot that this was a mistake, bad call, on his part. The cave was there, sure, but he didn't see anything inside, and besides, the opening was too small and that huge tree root was in the way. Sometimes you wrote shit like this off. He knew enough about history to know, or to feel that this wasn't stuff that should be sold anyway. He felt it when he was there. Sometimes these things just came to you. People who grow up here know this from when they're young—you don't fuck with stuff like this. Pinchot would understand that. Besides, it was all a shot in the dark from the beginning anyway. There was never any guarantee of anything.

When he got to Waikīkī he stood outside his car, wondering if he should call first. Phone calls seemed to irritate Pinchot, and he decided against it, and walked toward the building, going over in his mind how he would explain this.

Pinchot was not from Hawai'i and therefore didn't understand the importance of the kind of friendships that got formed and more or less cemented here. Pinchot did not know Derek, and did not know, therefore, how it felt to Billy, or William, to go through a calculated process of fucking over his friend's sister and the dude that way. It didn't matter that the guy was a sort of weirdo, a baseball-playing loner. Terry was a little on the weird side too, what with the ridiculous saying on her computer screen—do the dream dance—and what was the rest? With your body. Or with your body on? That was it. Then there was Flake Land.

When he got to Pinchot's door he paused again, took a deep breath, and pushed the little brass button.

Pinchot opened the door. "I thought I said tomorrow," he said, looking irritated. "Did you forget? We can't forget like that." The earring glinted in the light, his earlobe red.

"No, I didn't," he said. "It's the whole cave thing."

"All right," Pinchot said. "Come in."

He followed Pinchot to the living room. Through the window he could see the lights from a couple boats out in the bay mirrored on the water's surface.

"Well," Pinchot said, sitting down on the couch. "If you found the cave, what's the problem?"

"The problem is that it's a bad idea. I don't know if that stuff is in there or not, but I got a bad feeling when I was looking inside, you know, at that blackness."

"Didn't you have a flashlight? Come on."

"I did, but it was in my pocket and I had to climb to see in the cave. The opening is small because part of the roof of it collapsed."

"Then get some wood or something to hold it up and go inside."

"No, what I mean is the stuff in there doesn't belong to us. It—"

"William, what is this? It belongs to the person who finds it."

"I don't think so. You're from California, and maybe you don't understand."

"Oh, I'm liking this. What don't I understand?"

Billy prickled a little at his tone of voice. "Look," he said, "you know drugs are big here. I don't see any problem with that. This is a good way to make money, I know, but the business of raiding a cave somebody put Hawaiian things in all that time ago is wrong. I don't know if this guy who put it there was Hawaiian, but if he was, even one tenth, then this is a bad idea. It doesn't feel right, and I'm trying to explain that a person from California might not, like, tune into this idea. What I'm saying is that I can't go in there. Even if the opening was as big as that doorway, I wouldn't. It's just a bad idea. It doesn't feel right."

"Ah, mumbo jumbo then," Pinchot said. His phone rang. He picked it up, fingered the earring, listened, and said, "I assure you, it's a go. But you'll have to wait because the ship was delayed. I told you that." He listened. "Good, then we've got this square then." He hung up, turned back to Billy. "I don't think I need to remind you that I'm up to here in a debt I incurred unfairly. This discovery is one way out. Go back and get the stuff, and as I said, you'll be well compensated."

"I can't."

"You can't. Or you won't?"

"Both. I'm not going in the cave. Somebody else—"

"Spirits? Mana? Hocus pocus. Kids get scared of stuff like that. Kids and ignorant adults. Get over it."

Billy looked at the lights on the water. He was not a kid and he wasn't ignorant. "It's not ignorance," he said. "It's just being careful, a respectful whatchucall about this stuff. I don't like messing with this."

"This is business. In business we do what we have to do to get what we want. All that garbage about spirits and culture and auras and chants is all just that—garbage. It's a stupid fanaticism that you've bought into or that you grew up with that you have to shake off if you're going to do well. I see this shit on TV all the time and it makes me laugh. Jesus, people can be so stupid. Look, I'm trying to help you out here."

"Well, I don't think—"

"No, you don't think. I'll call a couple guys who'll go with you tomorrow and empty that fucking cave okay? I'll get somebody small who'll have the balls to crawl in there okay?"

"I don't think I'll go on that one."

"Yes you will," Pinchot said. "You will because I want you to. How many times do I have to explain this to you?"

"One time was enough," Billy said softly. The guy was not getting the point.

"No, you'll go, and tomorrow. I want that stuff and you'll be well compensated. I told you that. Now, I have work to do here."

Billy looked at the lights. "No," he said. "It's a bad idea and I can't do it. You have to understand how things are here."

Pinchot sighed, an exasperated release of breath, and got up from his leather couch. "Listen," he said, this time more softly. "You need at least to give us the information so that somebody who is not made into a chicken by the thought of a bunch of hogwash can do it. I'll still compensate you."

"It isn't hogwash and I'm not a chicken. You probably shouldn't say that. Out here you can get into trouble saying things like that to people. It's what we call 'talking stink', and—"

"Oh really," he said. "Really. I'm getting advice from you now? You work for me, asshole. You do what I say."

Billy shook his head. "You shouldn't do that, Mr. Pinchot. You really—"

Pinchot looked angry now. He walked around the coffee table following his index finger, which was pointed at Billy's face. "Just give us the information. You're beginning to get on my nerves, kid."

"Well, let's say you're getting on mines, too. Mine I mean."

"I'm telling you, you need to shape up. You need to get rid of this act. I thought we had a deal, a good one—" and he moved in closer, so that Billy backed away a little, his hands up. "—and you're screwing this up over a stupid superstition? What the fuck is this? Are you, what, a dumb moke after all? I want the information and you're going to give it to me. This is ridiculous. You dumb—"

He didn't realize he'd done it until Pinchot was lying on his back on the floor holding his nose, blood leaking on his cheeks. Billy stood there with his mouth open, and then stared at his fist, then looked down at Pinchot.

"Wait, I—"

"Oh boy," Pinchot said, sitting up and pulling an handkerchief out of his pocket and dabbing at his nose with it. "William, you're going to pay big time for this." He fumbled in his pocket for his cell phone while he held his nose wrapped in the handkerchief with the other.

"I'm sorry."

"Sorry, yeah. Asshole."

Billy stood there, looking down at him. Why did he call him that? He looked back toward the lights on the water, then down again at Pinchot. Then he felt light and weirdly airy, suddenly different. "Call um," he said. Pinchot studied the little keyboard, and he waited, staring down at him. He laughed softly. "Some cops hea my friens," he said. "Dey mokes too."

"You're going to pay, William. I want—"

"Billy, 'ass my name fucka. My name is Billy."

"You're going to pay."

"Yeah? Fo real? Who you like send fucka? You make one fucken army come ovah Kailua lookeen fo me? I get one too. One army of mokes dea, wipe da fucken street wit you guys. Go, call um."

"You'll pay."

"Yeah? How I pay ah? Fucka, what? I one stupid moke. Get pordagee an' flip blood, maybe t'ree dakines—" He snapped his fingers. "What is dat? Yeah. Platelets. Mus' get t'ree platelets Hawaiian blood too ah? Or else I wouldn't mumbo mumbo ah? I don't know. But you come. We kick yoa ass is what we do fucka. An' one nodda ting. If I stupid, I not stupid enough to owe somebody a million dollars. Dat's you brah. You da stupid one. An' plus, take dat fucken ring outta yoa ear. It sucks."

"William."

"Nah. Nah." He moved toward the door. "Billy. 'Ass my name, fucka. You like my address Kailua? I geev um to you an' we wait. You fuck wit' my friens you know what it means to pay brah, 'ass garans. We scrape yoa faces off onna street. But dis jus' talk ah? Moke talk. Come tes' um out, see if I booshitteen you. Try come, come Kailua, beef wit' us."

He left. Standing in the elevator, his heart pounding, he looked at his knuckles. He was shaking and his breath came in jerks. When the elevator opened on the ground floor, he walked out into a cool breeze and looked around. He felt light, exhilarated. Oh boy. That was it. He might have thought of her as crazy before, but not now. He might have stared at it and scratched his head and gone for years without ever figuring it out. But he had figured it out now. That was the dakine. The dream dance.

3:55 AM. Terry sat on the hood of a 1999 Honda Civic at the corner of the yard, listening to a rooster crow. She reached up and touched the bone hook *nice* and listened for the sound of Em's car. She'd worn the hook, at first, off and on, but as the days had passed, she began leaving it on, and in a dip into a new little personal insanity, she had been more and more reluctant to take it off. And now, she couldn't. If she walked out of the house without it her little voice said *no* and she would have to go back in and get it.

In her backpack she had her measuring cord, a clothesline at thirty yards, her snacks, a flashlight, water, and her screwdriver, perfect as a stake that they could put in the ground with the rope on it, the knot at thirty yards, then jerk the rope and pull it in and set the stake again.

She heard the sound of a car engine up on Keolu Drive, humming along in the rooster-interrupted silence and then slowing down, the shafts of headlight beams sweeping across windows up the street, and then Em's car pulled up. Four on the nose, and the door opened for her. She got in, feeling a little surge of fear *no, I like him, I do* at being with a guy at this time of the night. She put her hand up to touch the hook.

"So, ready?" he asked.

"Yup."

"I made coffee," he said. He turned the ceiling light on and pulled up an old thermos, and a plastic coffee cup with a faded duck on it. "Want some?"

"Yeah," she said, and he poured and gave her the cup. It was good, slightly flavored coffee.

"Lion," he said. "It's on sale at Longs."

"Oh."

"Three ninety-nine for the ten-ounce, which is good," he said. He poured coffee into the red cover of the thermos for himself. "Usually it's five ninety-nine. This one is the toasted coconut."

"Oh, that's—Yeah."

Then he drove, the lights sweeping by and tools slightly clacking in the back seat and the movement, a sort of floating that made her hold her breath *this is so fun* and taste the coffee, and she had this little flash of a sensation that there was no time, just them, floating, and she looked over at him sipping at his coffee as he drove. But things were such that any dream of being closer to him or anyone else was not really a possibility because in the delicate balance of the sane and the insane, the seesaw held perfectly level, preventing it. There had to be some other sign, some new thing to make any dream like that possible.

They were going up the Pali Highway, and would have to drive past the pull-off and parking for the trail and turn around farther up. Em did an illegal turn at an opening a few hundred yards beyond the trail, and floated back down the highway to the parking area.

"Well," he said, "I guess it's hiking in the dark."

"Is this too early, you think?"

"I don't know. The light starts in about an hour, so we'll be there by that time or a while after. I've got a good flashlight here."

"I have one, too."

They set off. At first she was frightened because the trail dropped into blackness downhill. Their flashlight beams bounced with their walking, making stretched-out X's when they were side by side, and other times she had to play it on the ground to keep from tripping over roots or rocks. The air was wet, thick; the trail smelled of mud and flowers and rotting fruit. She stayed as close to him as she could.

Their conversation was terse: "Oops, sorry," "Wow, look at the lights out there," "Oops," "Let's see, we've been walking thirty minutes," "Watch the roots right here," "Oops, sorry," "It's this gully here," "No, farther, I can picture it," "Oops."

As the sky began to lighten over Olomana and farther off against the hills along the ocean, she expected to see the gully up to the breadfruit tree. "Uh, let's see, this one?" "Yeah, that's it," "Oops, I don't think so."

When the sky had taken on a pink glow over the ocean, she saw it. "Here it is," she said. "Right here."

"Okay, so we—"

She went up through the grass, climbing past boulders and brush, and saw the top of the tree. "There it is," she said. Em came up the gully and stopped, looked at the tree. He looked at the ground around it.

"Someone's been here," he said. The grass was flattened. "I mean, we were. Did we stomp around on the grass a lot?"

"No, you heard the name of the tree and left."

"Well, I guess Ray was right. Let's do the measuring." He fiddled in his backpack and drew out a compass, an old one made of brass with a black needle turning inside, under glass.

"Where'd you get that?" she asked, squinting at it in the dawn light. The blue steel needle floated there under the glass.

"It's from the family. Old, maybe even Emiliano Gamez's, I don't know."

She had to climb back up the 30 yards only once to free the screwdriver. The measurement took them across the trail and then at a steep pitch down below the trail until they had marked out the 172 yards, and Em studied the compass to lay out the remaining yardage to where they would see the cave. The sun sent a pink and yellow fan of light over the small line of mountains near the ocean, and the peaks of Olomana Mountain, closer, remained a dark silhouette just a mile or so away.

Then, after the last 77 yards, they stood looking at a grassy wall of stone with vines and ferns along the top, just under where it tipped up to a steep angle back toward the trail. "It's here somewhere," Em said. "I'd say up on that rock face."

There were a couple of muddy swipes in the grass at the bottom. "Someone's been here, too," he said.

She looked around, feeling uneasy. Was that somebody still here *no* in the bushes? Em went to the base of the rock face and grabbed grass, trying to pull himself up. "I'd say it's behind the ferns," he said. "Maybe you could stand on my shoulders."

She took her backpack off. "Okay, how do I do this?"

He laced his fingers together to form a kind of stirrup for her foot.

"I'll hoist, you grab grass up above, and then you can step up on my shoulders."

She felt strange about doing this, so physically close, but put her backpack on the ground and walked over to him. He still had his fingers laced, and she placed her left foot in them, put her hands on his shoulders, and felt herself rise right up, and stepped on his shoulders, grabbed fern and looked at it. It was uluhe, or *Dicranopteris linearis*. Then she put her right hand through, felt rock, then a space, then the bark of a tree, then a large space. "More left," she said. He did so. She would have to do an awkward chin-up in order to see the space. "Can you push me up another foot? I feel space."

"Uh, well—"

"What?"

"It's like, where I have to put my hand?"

"Oh." She looked at the fern. "Go ahead. Make believe I'm a cheerleader."

"Well—"

"No, go ahead."

She felt his hand on her buttocks, and rose, so that now she could move the fern away with one hand. "Cave," she said. "The way in is small."

"Okay." She heard a physical tension in his voice, felt a buzz of tension in his hand.

"You getting tired?"

"No, keep looking."

"Do you have your flashlight?"

"Can't," he said.

She put both hands on the lip of the opening and pulled up, away from his hand, and braced her feet on some little cluster of roots, enough to hold herself there. "Get the flashlight," she said.

"You okay up there?"

"Yeah, go ahead."

She heard him down below, a zipper zipped, and then he tapped the light on her shoe. "Can you reach down?" he asked.

She could, and drew the flashlight up, and pulled herself further toward the opening, felt his hands now on the bottoms of her sneakers. She turned the flashlight on, and aimed it into the hole.

It was silt that sloped down and away, and the back of it was fifteen feet or more away, a rock wall, dry and hazed by spider webs. In the foreground the silt dipped. "Silt," she said.

"What?"

Her voice had been stolen by that blackness, a muffled, echoless sound to it. When she moved her head farther in and felt the cool dry air *this is fun, go in* she found it easy to pull her body through the narrow opening, hearing behind her Em's voice—hey, you shouldn't—

She saw what had happened—the ceiling of the cave had fallen, like flaps of a box, and in the gap where the rock had split was a thick root, probably a tree root, and the root back to her right stood as a pillar of sorts. She began to feel breathless, as if it might crush her at any moment *go farther, this is fun, go go* and kill her. She moved over the silt like a snake, feeling the roof of the cave scrape her back, and played the light around. Silt. "Silt," she said back toward the light. She felt the bone hook dragging in the silt and stuffed it inside her T-shirt.

"You shouldn't go in there," he called.

"Can you give me the screwdriver?" she called back over her shoulder.

There was scraping, thumps, then a hand on her sneaker. She felt back, saw the sunlight in the yellow handle.

"Terry?"

"Yeah, let me get—"

She twisted around and got the screwdriver. He was chinning himself on the lip of the cave, his face a black silhouette, and then he slipped. And then the thump.

"You okay?" she called.

"Yeah, but—"

She put her head down on her forearm and got her breath, shining the flashlight on the ceiling looking for bugs. The silt was fine and hard, dry and as flat as a pool table where she was lying, and then planed downward as it went deeper into the cave. She moved ahead and got on her side, set the flashlight down so that the beam ran across her hands, and drove the blade of the screwdriver into the silt, which broke easily, so that she could cup handfuls out and throw them farther into the cave.

"What are you doing?" he called.

"Digging."

The opening darkened again. He was chinning himself.

"I'll be out in a bit," she said. "I'm just digging here. You can wait. I'm okay. I'm digging."

"Uh, okay," he said, and his face dropped away. "I'm not sure this is a good idea," he called from below.

She kept digging, her hands strangely bright in the beam of the light, the intensity of it going through her fingertips like an X-ray so that they were reddish, the hands of someone else digging.

There was a pause, then, like when they were driving in the dark and time stopped. It stopped again, and she felt herself, her body settling and relaxing, comfortably prone on the silt, sound itself enclosing her, almost as if she were dozing off, going to sleep here. But she was digging, languidly and mechanically moving silt farther back into the cave. The deeper she went the softer and less packed it was. She looked at the closer wall, stopped digging, and played the flashlight beam over the rough, black stone. If she were storing stuff in a cave, she would probably put it next to a wall rather than in the middle. She set the flashlight down aimed at the wall. She began pulling silt from the wall and into the hole she had dug. She was lost in a pleasant fog, her fascination with the cool darkness reducing sound and taking away her sense of what she was doing or why she was doing it. She pulled silt from the wall, stirred silt with the screwdriver, cupped more away.

Her eyes had adjusted to the darkness, and when she saw a diminishing light, she looked back to see Em chinning himself again, but she said nothing because now she was digging and there was nothing to say.

"You okay?"

"I'm digging."

The silhouette disappeared. She turned back to her work *good* and continued digging. Why she felt that serene isolation, she didn't know. She dug. The silt came up like sugar, handful after handful. In her weird and tranquil distraction from everything, she forgot what she was looking for because the silt felt like sugar and she thought, what is wrong with me? What is *nothing* wrong?

Her fingertips slid on something smooth and round. She stopped, wormed her fingers, and felt it again, round and the size of a grapefruit, wood, and she slid her fingers over the dome and levered it side to side in the sugar, the lower part of it knocking against what sounded like wood on each side. Clunk clunk clunk. It rose in small increments, clunk by clunk, and then she pulled it out, the wooden figurine raining silt, its two shell eyes looking at her. She held her breath, drew it toward her, hearing somewhere a hissing sound, then strange, remote and faint chattering, of tiny faraway voices, children a hundred yards away—wind across the cave opening, she was sure—but she couldn't pull her eyes away from the two off-white shells, and she stared, the distant chatter just beyond her ability to make out words, and finally she let out her breath, blowing silt off the wooden face in a puff. She had no impulse to move yet *get out* but the ticklish *let's get out* pull of her will told her to slide around and get back out, because she now began to feel the small, jerky beginning of a claustrophobic panic taking hold. It was time to move now, to get out. Everything was too close. And then she pictured her room, boxes, a computer screen, a bed, the drawer, and she saw the bottle of Cutty and the boxes of cold medicine and the panic intensified *get out* and the picture, multiplying in her imagination now into dozens of boxes and green bottles with the elliptical circle of air dancing and undulating in each one, and they continued to multiply, boxes and more boxes and bottles and that circle dancing, and the revulsion and panic she felt ballooned throughout her flesh *it's time* and she reached for the flashlight and screwdriver, her hand numb and trembling.

She slid her body around, holding the wooden image and the flashlight and screwdriver against her chest, now feeling two wooden points against her ribs—breasts on the image, and started snaking her way to the bright opening, and as she approached it, her heart pounding and her breath coming in truncated jerks, she wanted to fly out of it, the light intensifying and hurting her eyes. She moved into the opening, the light blinding her, and said, "I—out. Let me out," and she slid out of the opening and pivoted around, and then lowered herself down the muddy face of the bank, over grass tufts, to the ground where Em caught her.

"You okay?" he asked.

"Huh?"

"Are—" Then he saw the wooden figure. "Wow, look at that."

She held it out to him. In the light, her eyes adjusting, she saw that one side of the figure was gray, as if exposed to weather over a long period of time. The flashlight was still on, a faint orange in the bright light. She turned it off.

"It was down in the silt," she said. She was still a little stunned by the light, looking at him as he studied the statue. "There are others."

"I wouldn't go back in there," he said. He sounded a little breathless. "No way. You should stay out. I was looking at this—" He pointed up at the wooden pillar made by the tree root. "—and that's what's holding the rock up. I—"

"It's—I mean, there's not much room. I—"

"Yeah, don't go in. I don't—Are you going to try that again?"

"No."

"Okay, good."

"Yeah."

"Not a good idea."

"I know."

He looked around, thinking. The ocean was bright, white lines of surf partway out, clouds in the distance.

"Uh, what do you want to do now?" he asked.

"I don't know."

"I'll take you to breakfast, how's that sound?"

"Okay."

He stared at her.

"Are you, uh, okay?"

"Yeah."

"We have to figure out what to do. Maybe nothing. I mean it's—"

"It's—"

"It's maybe what—Well, we can figure something out."

"Okay. It was like sugar."

"We can—" He stared. "What was like sugar?"

"The silt."

"Oh."

"Sound was funny. My body—"

He stared. "Your body?"

"I mean, sound was funny."

He looked again at the wooden figure. "So it was real," he said.

"Real?"

"Everything was real. It's all really in there, but—" He looked out toward the ocean.

"But?"

"I don't like it. The part up there that's caved in. Maybe—Hey, look, we get a fruit picker, okay?"

"A fruit picker. Okay."

"We make like a little shovel for the end."

"Okay. A shovel. Okay."

"We pass it in there and dig in the sugar. I mean silt. You said it was like sugar, right?"

"I did. I did say that."

"And we pull the sugar—I mean the silt out, and then when we get something—" He stopped, looked away. "Unearthed, that's it. When we get something unearthed, we make a little noose and pass it in."

"Okay."

"You see what I mean?"

"I am hungry though. I just realized that."

"Yeah." He looked at the cave opening. "I'll pick up some stuff. Steel tape measure, you know, the kind that we can—"

"Yellow."

"Huh?"

"The tape. It's yellow."

"Yeah."

"A lot of tools are yellow."

"That's right."

He looked around, thinking. "Okay, I'll put this in my backpack," he said, looking at the wooden statue. He went to the backpack, unzipped it, and slid the statue inside as far as he could, the head with the two shell eyes above the top of the pocket looking toward the back, the two pointy breasts making star-shaped lumps in the thick, blue fabric. He put the backpack on.

"Whaddaya think?" he asked.

"Okay." She put her backpack on.

They made their way up the bank in the morning sunlight. When they were on the trail, he led the way so that the two shell eyes looked back at her, and she found herself locking her eyes in on them and the eyes' rhythm, bouncing there on his back, became a slow, weird dance that mesmerized her so that she stumbled over roots, had to force herself to look away, down to where her feet went, and as in the cave when the eyes looked at her and she thought of her room, she thought of her room again and thought, my god that's awful. I've got to pour it out. As soon as I get home I've got to pour it out.

They walked. It seemed to take three times as long as the trip in. The shell eyes looked at her and they walked.

When they emerged at the trail parking area, Em turned. "Still hungry?"

"Yeah."

They wiped mud off their clothes, put the backpacks on the tools in the car.

"I'll still get mud on your seats," she said.

"Don't worry about the seats," he said.

They got in his car. Other cars were pulling in, one a Mercedes. "More hikers," he said. "Rich ones."

She didn't understand. Then she worked on the words, and thought, oh, he means hikers who have money.

She suspected that it would not be a good day when, at the parking area, she saw an old car leave, and thought that it looked like Em Lindross's. Then, shortly afterward, another car pulled in, a Mustang, and two men got out and came to Hal Kraft's window, not exactly dressed for hiking. Board shorts on one, regular dress pants on the other, golf shirts, and both wearing tennis shoes. They were his workers, security, and odd job performers he used on occasion, he said. The one in long pants had two fingers missing from his left hand, the pinky and the ring finger, and also had a flat, lethally vacant look about him. Hal introduced them as Ken and Wes. Ken was a more or less amiable thug, while Wes looked at her and said nothing. His expression didn't even change. There was something faintly creepy about him, the look of his hand with two fingers opposed by a thumb, oddly resembling the chrome device you'd see where an entire hand was missing.

And George—she was not sure that he would be able to process the orders she gave him, three times. He kept asking her to repeat, and she had to tell him to lower the cell phone a little on his ear so that he could hear. Yes ma'am, I know where this trail is. But she did not see his little car, that rusted Tercel she placed notes on.

As they walked, Hal with his fingers in backpack straps, looking around and asking again and again if Ken and Wes were sure this here wasn't the right gully, Natalie wondered more and more about the wisdom of going on a hike with the three of them. She found herself looking around at brush, up gullies and so on, expecting to see George, and then realized that she was tipping her hand if one of them should see her looking and wonder why. In any case her instructions were clear: do not call on the cell. Keep an eye on us, and if anything happens, appear. Sweet and myopic as he was, the Hulk was a formidable looking man. And then there was the other car at the lot. She decided not to mention that the car leaving could have been Em Lindross's. She decided to leave the business of doing this to the expert of sorts.

In ways this game had become tiresome, not because she was any less interested in the prize, but because of all the bullshit the whole thing was causing. Ray and his whining self-righteous condemnation of her trying to score when there was a chance. She was tired of it, tired of his trying to heap the oh-so-moral guilt trip on her. Fuck him. She'd gotten up in the morning and dug in the closet for her hiking boots, which she hadn't worn in years, and he had watched her from the bed, probably hung over, speaking in that same deliberately sarcastic tone he had used the previous evening: "Hiking ought to be good this time of year."

"I'm sure it is," she'd said, working the laces around the clips and pulling her socks up. "It's quite beautiful, I'm sure."

"So you're assuming the loser hasn't been up there yet."

"I'm assuming nothing," she'd said.

"Would you like me to make coffee?"

"No, I'll pick one up at Starbucks."

"Ah, Starbucks."

He wouldn't drop that tone.

"Look," she'd said, "I'm doing this for us, get it? Just get up, make yourself a drink, and relax. I haven't time for this banter."

"All right," he'd said. "But I have to go to work today. I can't make myself a drink."

"I'll be back later. I have to wait outside for my ride."

"All right."

That wasn't a good start. And now she was walking into a remote area with three people who did not look like hikers, except perhaps for Hal, who wore chino pants stuffed into the tops of his boots, and resembled a refugee from some forties movie set in Africa, *King Solomon's Mines* or something like that. A bad imitation of Stewart Granger. It was quite ridiculous. But it would not be if they scored. The possibility that the old car leaving was Em's, of course, put a damper on the likelihood of that. She imagined the dumb shit with all that loot. Would he even know what to do with it? Probably not.

It was really quite beautiful in the sun, the broad panorama of Kailua laid out on their left. She imagined that if she had a telescope, she'd be able to see some of the very houses she had listed and was now unfortunately neglecting, what with all the mental energy going into this.

Ahead they had stopped. The thugs were pointing up the hill, actually up a gully, and Hal pulled a tape measure out of his pocket. Then he pulled out a pad and studied one of the pages, turned and looked down the bank. Then his face went sour. "God damn," he said.

"What?" she asked.

"Someone's been here," he said, pointing at the bank. She looked. There were gouges in the dirt.

"That doesn't mean someone's been at the cave."

"Ken," he said. Ken turned from the gully. "Take this to the tree and measure down. You go too, Wes." The thugs went up the gully.

"Well, we'll see," she said.

They could then hear the twanging of the tape as the guys stretched out and let it back in. Finally they got to the trail, Wes walking with the steel tape behind him. "Twenty," he called up. Then Ken appeared, holding the yellow device out before him as he drew the tape back in. "Seventy-one," he said, pointing at his foot.

"Okay, did you use the compass?"

"Yup."

"The dirt is gouged right on line with the compass," he said. "This may be going south on us right now." The look on his face was weird—irritated and almost furious without even any proof that anything was going south. Or west, or anywhere.

"Do we go on?" Ken asked.

"Yes," Hal said.

They made their way down the steep bank, Hal very gingerly working his way over the grass and rocks, as if he didn't want to get his clothes messed up. It was enough of a pitch that she had to work her way carefully, too, or she would end up on her ass. When the thugs were done with their measuring, they moved to a flatter shelf, Hal looking into the compass to find the next direction. The guys just stood there waiting for their instructions, looking out over Kailua and the ocean.

"Okay, it's this way, seventy-seven yards, but I see tramped grass. We'll just follow the tracks I suppose."

He seemed now to have tired of the whole thing, and so had she. If Em had emptied the cave, what was the use? The game was over. But if the cave was full of this stuff, how could Em carry it all out? He'd have to make a number of trips. And on his first, you could easily imagine he'd go for the doubloons before worrying about useless wooden statues, weapons, and shit like that.

She followed as the three made their way along a side of a fairly steep bank, and then stopped and looked around. Here they were somewhat out of view of the trail, and she looked around, again wondering if George was watching.

"There it is," Hal said. He was looking up at a small cliff face that had a thick growth of ferns on it, one part opened up so that a black hole in the rock face was visible. The thug named Ken backed up and took a couple of preliminary hops, and jumped up and grabbed thick grass, and then reached up and got one hand on the lip of the opening. Hanging there, he looked back. "Too small," he said. "But it looks like someone's done something here."

"Done what?" Hal asked.

"It's full of dirt, and there are, like, gouges in it."

"Oh that's good," Hal said. "If it's too small, as you say, then what did they do, send a kid in there?"

Ken slid back down the face, and wiped his hands. "Too small for me anyway," he said. "But it's like a flat plane of dirt, right at eye level, all the way back maybe fifteen to twenty feet."

"Silt," Hal said. "So most of the artifacts would still be there, under the silt." He stepped closer. "If the opening is so small, how did he get the stuff in there?"

Ken went back up. Wes watched from below, his left hand in his pocket.

"It's collapsed in the middle," Ken said, hanging on the lip. "There's a thick root right here," and he pulled aside some of the fern. The root was about eight inches thick, from the ceiling edge to the lip.

"So we cut the root out," Hal said.

"Then the roof might collapse."

"That hole looks big enough for a person," Hal said. "Can you get inside?"

"Not enough room in there."

Hal was becoming agitated, it appeared, as if the hole were some slight against him. "Can't you just climb in?"

"Nope."

Hal looked at Wes. He was a lot smaller than Ken. "Can you go up and look?"

Wes looked at him, his eyes flat, and went to the base of the cliff. Then he quite easily scaled it, until he was next to Ken, who slid back down, allowing Wes to pull himself across and to the hole, the strange claw-like left hand apparently just as strong as his right. He peered into the hole, turned and shook his head.

"Give it a try," Hal said.

Wes pulled himself up, and worked at getting his shoulders through, wedged himself side to side, and had the top half of his body inside. Then he wedged himself out. "No," he said.

"You were in," Hal said. "Just go in, okay?"

"No."

"What's the matter? I saw you all the way in except for your hips and legs, man. Just go in."

He slid down the face and brushed his hands off, then his pant legs. He did this slowly and deliberately. He was not going back up.

"C'mon," Hal said. "Just go in. It's safe."

"No."

"When you looked inside," Hal asked Ken, "did you see the silt and the ceiling?"

"Well, it opens up a little inside."

Hal stared at Wes with a kind of amiable perplexity.

"So Wes, what do you think?"

"No."

Hal looked down the mountain toward the buildings spread out along the ocean, then at the clouds illuminated by the morning sunlight. He looked back. "What's the problem?"

"There's no problem. Just not goin' in."

Hal sighed, looked at his watch. "Hm. Well, does that make you a—let me see, I should use your terminology I think. He says there's room in there and you say you don't want to go in. Does that make you a pussy?"

"Oops," Natalie whispered.

Ken smiled and then quickly gritted his teeth in sympathy for poor Wes, the little pussy.

"C'mon now Wes," Hal said. "You're chickening out on me. You're being a pussy. Just go in there. We'll be here."

Wes didn't respond. He began brushing his pant legs again. Then he stopped, stood up straight, and looked at Kailua and the ocean. She felt briefly sorry for the boy, as if she suddenly had perceived him as a hungry refugee or an orphan.

"Wes," Hal said, "we can't stand here all day. Just go in and look around and come back out. It's clear that we've got to go for some tools, maybe a hatchet or something to cut out that root—"

"Not sure about that," Ken said.

"I'm not talking to you now," Hal said flatly to him. Ken shrugged and smiled with amiable helplessness, and turned to Wes, who continued looking flat-faced at the ocean.

"Well," Hal said. "We've reached an impasse here. We've found the cave—that is clear. We've isolated both the problem—" and he pointed at the cave entrance, "—and the solution, which is you, Wes. Now we have to go the next step."

"No," Wes said softly. "Do it another way."

"There is no other way right now," Hal said. "Yes, maybe you feel a little closed in? But we'll be out here. Just go up there and crawl in, just as I saw you do a minute ago."

"No."

"But the sunlight goes right in—it'll be light in there. We'll talk you through it. All I want you to do is call out some, well, findings. I want you to push a stick into the silt to see how deep it is."

"Hal," she said, "maybe we should do this another way. It's clear that he doesn't want to go in there, and—"

"He'll do it," Hal said. "He works for me." He turned to Wes, and said, "You told me back in Seattle that you 'ain't afraid of nothing,' did you not?"

Wes looked at Kailua and the ocean.

"So now you prove it, okay? Very simple—we want some information about the cave, you are the key to that information."

"Not doin' it," Wes said.

"Then you are afraid of something, or shall we say, 'somethin'.'"

Wes looked at him with that same flat, dead stare, and began walking through the grass toward the spot that led up to the trail.

"Wes," Hal called. "C'mon. Come back."

Wes kept going.

Hal sighed. "I've apparently hurt his feewings," he said.

Ken smiled, shrugged, and looked at Natalie. It seemed that the whole thing was funny to him.

"Well let's see," Hal said. "Here I have what? Some rope, a couple small tools. I'll work at making a ladder of sorts." He looked into his bag, then around at the brush and natural debris. "Ken, here's what we do—you hike out, catch up with Wes, and you two go into Kailua and buy, say, a small hatchet. We'll hack that root out so that someone with more bravery can go on in there. In fact, I'll do it." He looked up the bank, thinking, then pulled his car keys out of his pocket. "If he goes somewhere else and you can't find him, take my car." He flipped the keys to Ken, who made his way quickly toward the trail.

Natalie was left there with Hal, which made her feel a little better, although she wondered now if George would see this as an excuse to come out of the brush. While Hal went down the bank and pulled at a long branch from a dead tree, she looked around for George, and thought of that pitiful kid Wes, and wondered about Hal's nastiness. He was worse than she was.

He was still a little shaken by it, and sitting there with Terry across from him at the downtown Kailua McDonald's, he thought, stupid—that was stupid, letting her go in there like that. He had stood there with his breath held, waiting for that rock ceiling to cave in, and when she finally had come out, blinking and stunned, he could finally breathe, and thought, no, no, never again. He would never again set himself up to be responsible for another person's death, so long as he lived. All the doubloons in the world weren't worth that.

She burped. "Oops," she said. She was eating her second breakfast burrito doused with mild sauce.

"You must have some pretty radical metabolism," he said. "Didn't you eat breakfast already?"

"Uh huh," she said. "Cereal, a banana, two granola bars, and a plum." She thought a moment. "And V8 Juice and a multiple vitamin, and a calcium tablet." She thought more. "Plus something else, I forgot."

"Jesus."

"If you don't eat right, you're hash."

"Okay."

"Your—You can't be like, on, when you don't eat right."

"Okay." Now he wondered if he should have ordered two of those burritos. "Well, look, I'd like to go back, maybe measure, and work on a tool of some sort."

"Okay."

"But I don't want you to go back in the cave."

"Okay."

"It isn't worth it."

"Okay."

He looked at her as she made her way to the folded, doughy base of the burrito. Could he talk to her? He wondered. He wanted to say something about other stuff, like the way she affected him, wanted somehow to say something that would go past the various what? Barriers? He couldn't figure her out. And he guessed he didn't have the guts to say, well, anything really personal to her. He wished he could, but he was who he was.

"Well, maybe we should go back and do this, and just see. It's amazing that you pulled out the statue—it means it's all true."

"I guess it does."

"And there are still doubloons to consider."

"Okay."

"I mean, assuming they're there."

"Okay."

"So—"

"Okay."

They slid out of the booth.

As they drove through Kailua, he talked again about the cave. "You said that the one you pulled out was knocking against others, so, if we put the tape measure in, we can make a tool."

"Okay."

"And do everything from the outside. If I push you up there, you won't go back in, right?"

"No."

"It isn't worth it."

"No."

He wasn't sure if he believed her. She had simply slithered in without hesitating, driven by some odd or obsessive curiosity rather than a logical response to an obvious danger. What was the word? Willful, maybe. Those two muddy sneakers just shot right in there, and right away he had seen how obvious the danger was.

"Because of traffic I have to go all the way up to come back."

"Okay."

He drove along to the peaceful rattle of tools. They passed the parking lot, saw four cars there, and drove on. To turn around legally he had to go into the road to the Pali lookout, and take the Kailua ramp out to go back down the mountain. When they got to the parking lot, he sat thinking about what they needed. The backpacks were in the trunk. They were about an hour from the tree.

"Maybe we just take the tape measure," he said. "And we try measuring, maybe take a piece of paper and a pen?"

"I have that," she said.

"Because we aren't going in. We're measuring, right?"

"Uh huh."

"Do we need water?"

"No, don't need water."

Hm, should he take the chance? She sat there ready to go, that weird contemplative look on her face. Well, he could always grab her foot if she tried.

They made their way into the trail. Not burdened by his backpack, he picked up round stones and selected targets. Terry looked around. "Okay," she said. "The dead tree on the right. That way you can't damage any bark."

He wound up and winged at it. The stone bounced off and down the bank.

"Strike," she said.

"Okay, this will be a sidearm fastball." He threw it, and it hit the tree with an impressive "pock!"

"So are you going back to college?" she asked.

"I don't know. First I have to deal with the apartment. My sister wants to sell it and I guess right now I don't." He didn't know if it would be any use to explain it, but went on. "I don't know what it'll sell for, but the principal we owe is pretty high. The profit wouldn't be much. And besides, these days, if you own something, you probably should try to keep it."

"Probably," she said.

"So the only advantage is that we owe so much on it that, what with the profit being low, I was thinking I'd try to offer her some money and keep it."

"You probably should keep it."

They continued walking, and he picked up three more stones. "That's why I'm doing all the gardening stuff."

"Landscaping, it's called," she said.

"So it's like, I don't spend any money. I put it in the bank and figure if I can hold her off, maybe—"

"What you do is buy CDs and get the interest, too."

"A CD is one of those things?"

"Like five percent," she said. "So if it's a thousand dollars, it's fifty dollars a year."

He stopped. She bumped into him from behind. "Sorry," he said. He was thinking, if a thousand gets fifty, then his eleven thousand would get—"Five hundred fifty dollars," he said. "At least on the eleven thousand I have."

"Right, and the next year it would be more."

"That's called compounding, right?"

"That's what it's called."

"Well, let's go."

"Okay."

Another fifty yards in, where the trail dropped somewhat sharply into a ravine, they traversed the bottom and looked up to see a guy walking out with a knife in his right hand, a little more than fifty feet away.

"Oops," Terry said.

"Hm," he said. The guy walked with a wooden determination, the knife in one hand and his left hand in his pocket, his face glazed and angry. Em's scalp prickled, and he set a stone in his crooked fingers. Then another guy appeared, and said, "Wes, hey Wes!"

The man with the knife stopped, turned to look at the other man, who had stopped when he saw the knife. Then the first man turned back, and looked flatly at them, the knife still in his hand. Em calculated where they were, looked back once at the terrain. It was steep behind them, steep ahead, a sharp drop-off on their left, too steep on the right. He didn't know how fast Terry could run.

"Pick a target," he said to Terry.

"What?"

"Pick a target."

She looked around. "The tree over there?"

"No, loud, enough for him to hear."

"Tree stump," she said, loud. "Over there."

He wound up and threw. The stump was so rotted that the stone vanished into it, spraying mulchy wood out.

"Another," he said. The two men watched.

"The rock over there."

It was about sixty-five feet away. Perfect. He wound up and threw, and the stone hit it and went up in an impressive arc, a good thirty feet. He looked around on the ground under him and found two more stones, and stood up straight, bouncing one in his hand.

"We get the point," the second man said.

"You going out?" Em called, hefting the stone. He had hit both targets, and felt reasonably confident. It was like baseball—when you were on, you were on, and there was no pressure, just the sure sense of targets and a simple explosive motion. It felt like elevated blood pressure, that confidence. He had known the feeling since he was twelve. It calmed him as he stood there bouncing the rock in his hand. He waited.

"Yeah, if you just hold up there," the guy said.

"We'll move up here," Em said. "Otherwise, no problem, just another day, rain maybe." Why had he said that? He put his hand on Terry's shoulder and she grabbed saplings and pulled her way up a dirt bank, and he followed, then found a place where he could turn back to the men.

The one with the knife watched, and then walked with that same determined, wooden gait, the other following with an apologetic smile on his face. "Sorry," he said to Em and Terry, and then followed the other man. "Hey Wes?" he said, but the other walked on, ignoring him. When they were gone he relaxed, dropped the stones. Terry looked at the space where they had vanished, her mouth open.

"You okay?" he asked.

"I—Yes."

"Well, I guess we can go on."

"What was that about, do you think?"

"No way of knowing," he said.

When they were back on the trail, Em sighed. "Well," he said, "let's just hang on here a second. I'm just not sure about who's on the trail today. But I don't want that guy cutting my tires or trying to get in the trunk of the car. What do you think?"

"Let's buy Mrs. Ikeda's trees," she said.

Trees? What trees? Then he remembered. "Oh, yeah. Okay."

"We need them, remember?"

"Okay."

Everything was darker, tinged by a purple haze, and he felt the two fingers throbbing there in his pocket. Everything was purple. He had taken the knife out thinking of slashing the Mercedes tires but that wasn't killing him. He had to kill him and that would mean going back but people would see. He had to wait. He didn't like nature anyway. He liked right angles. Painted things. Air conditioning.

But the vision came to him when he got into the car. The vision was beautiful, its logic coming to him like a high definition time-lapse sunrise. There were different ways of dying. Different ways of killing. Chopping fingers off only made the victim smarter. That was why things seemed purple. Ken was standing there trying to get him to go to that town to get a saw. No. I got stuff to do, he said up to Ken's purple face.

Ken left in the Mercedes, drove down the hill to look for a hardware store. As he sat, the guy and girl came back out of the trail, looked over in his direction, got into an old beater of a car and left. Then he started the car.

Kailua was a pretty town, tinged purple. He drove through it to the beach road and toward the part of town Mr. Kraft lived in, and once there, recalled the road that went up to the huge house overlooking the water and the two islands. It went past a canal and then a restaurant and then into a single-lane loop, and he drove slowly until he saw the road that went up, and drove in, found the house. He parked in the carport. There was an entry there, and he paused, recalling that the security system was not yet activated. He tried the door. It was locked. He went around and up a steep bank to the upper section, and tried a sliding door. Locked. He looked at his watch—he probably had an hour. He went back to the carport. Tried cupboards and locker. One was open, and inside was a black plastic suitcase with yellow battery-operated hand tools. He took out a drill, put the battery in the handle, and drilled a hole in the door, then took what he thought was called a sawzall, with its high-speed blade mounted in the nose, and put the blade in the hole and sawed a man-sized hole in the door, the saw vibrating his hands, fine sawdust falling on his sneakers. Then, carrying the saw and the drill, he went inside. The purple was fading and everything was starting to become clear.

The idea took its full form then: Mr. Kraft had said it—it's what the human being does with his tools that counts. The human being is nothing, just flesh and weakness, but oh what he can do with his tools. He went up a short flight of stairs into a kitchen anteroom. Canned goods. Olives. He went into the kitchen. A large mask—what? New Guinea. He pulled it from the wall and sawed it in half, bored holes in it. He went to the living room. More masks. A large Chinese porcelain pot—he broke it with the handle of the drill.

The good stuff was back from the living room, in rooms off the halls. In the first room, gold glassware, and silver stuff, tiny cups cradled in silver baskets. This would be that special glass, like the gold lamps and vases Mr. Kraft had shown him in Seattle. These he put on the floor and crushed with the heel of his sneaker. The gold glass—some name—Breakfast at. Tiffany, that was it. He carefully and meticulously broke them all, leaving a spectacular patch of gold and silver and iridescent rubble on the cork floor. The purple was almost gone. He didn't feel the fingers. The two left gripped the handle of the drill. He went to the next room. It was air conditioned, which he appreciated because he'd begun to sweat. All the objects inside required a cool atmosphere: old books, oil paintings, engravings. He slashed the high-speed blade of the saw through beautiful nature scenes, idyllic islands, the faces of stern people of old. He pulled large, leather-bound books off the shelves and drilled them full of holes. There were weird photographs on silver and glass, which he drilled, broke under his heel, bent and folded in half. There was a large, old camera whose body was of some fine-grained wood. He sawed it in half. He paid careful, diligent attention to the objects in the room, working with a methodical force. When he was done he went to the next room.

It glittered with fine glass and porcelain all laid out on wooden shelves. One by one he broke them until the floor was an inch deep with shards of glass and fine china, their blue and pink decorations mixed in with the glitter of the glass.

In another air conditioned room he found weapons, muskets and swords and clubs and blowguns and thin brightly decorated spears and flintlock pistols. He sawed musket stocks in half, and when the saw battery ran down he blocked a chair in an open door and in the crack levered muskets around and bent their barrels. He broke the thin spears, he broke blades of samurai swords and naval officers' swords and a nice Nazi hunting knife.

He decided that he did not need the drill any more and took its eighteen-volt battery and put it in the handle of the saw. There was another smaller room, but it was empty but for shelves and an old desk. He opened the drawer, and inside was a pretty bowl with a top. There was a mirror and a razor. He put the top of the bowl on the floor and broke it, and saw white powder inside, and next to it, farther back in the drawer, a straw. He left that alone. While you are contemplating man's work with his tools, snort some of this. He placed the bowl on the floor and stood the straw up in the powder, and then sawed the table in half.

Having finished the four main rooms in the back, he made his way toward the living room. He decided to leave the objects there intact. In another room off the dining area he found beautiful furniture made of something he thought they called koa and sawed it—lopped arms off chairs, cut the inlaid front panel of a drop-down desk top in half, cut off the legs, ran the blade through the back slats of a rocking chair and lopped the rockers in half, cut a wooden inlaid picture of a beach scene in half, reduced a very fine table to kindling, and ran the battery out cutting a large coffee table in half.

He left that room and opened a cupboard. Inside was a fancy silver teapot that he put on the floor and stomped nearly flat. Staring at it, he had his next vision, and it was startling, so beautiful that he thought there must be some message in it, some great point to be made.

He pulled out his wallet. There were lessons to be learned, that was it. He was nearly done here. He went to the living room, to Mr. Kraft's phone. It sat on a large glass coffee table. He used the handle of the saw to break off one part of the table, and then felt ashamed—that was cheap. Bush league. Oh well. He pulled out his card. The airline numbers were on it. He dialed one, and then had to stand, poke buttons, wait, until he began to wonder if he should be doing this somewhere else.

Then he got someone. "I need to book a flight to Los Angeles right away, if that's possible." It was. He booked a first class seat for the evening flight under his own name, reading out his credit card numbers to the very helpful lady on the other end. The flight was for 8:10, and he had an e-ticket. This he would not use.

The idea of Mr. Kraft's showing up now bothered him, but he buried that, because if Mr. Kraft showed up he would die, bleed to death gazing at the works of humans. It would be a disappointment, but that was the way things were. The man would not get the point. He dialed up another airline, one that served Seattle, and pulled the materials out of his wallet, a driver's license, social security card, and other cards belonging to a Reverend Richard Wilcox, the ID and social security numbers good enough not to raise any suspicion. He stood at the large window listening to a song by that guy brother something or other, or "braddah" something, "and think to myself, what a wonderful world," and thought that maybe he did like nature, those two beautiful little islands sitting out there in that blue water, red and yellow kayaks and canoes cutting through it, palm trees just below him. The song went on. He picked up the saw and idly broke another piece off the coffee table, and stared at the foot-long shard of glass on the floor, considered sawing the legs off another smaller table in the corner, but then he wouldn't be able to hear. He didn't have a fresh battery anyway. So he walked across the room to the glass-doored shelves he had planned to leave alone, and passed the time shattering fine china and glassware, making sure to keep his ear on the phone.

Here is your lesson, Mr. Kraft. You will see this demonstration of a human being's work with his tools. You will call the police, who will of course anticipate one Wesley Cotton's departure and they will conclude that, the ticket not being used, Mr. Cotton is still on this island. In the meantime the Reverend Richard Wilcox will be on his way to Seattle, on his way to the mother lode of the human being's works, where the Reverend will become Wesley Cotton, who will continue the lesson with the same careful dedication, no, with even more care and thoroughness, and oh my god what a job that will be, what a masterpiece of the human being's work!

Listening to another song, and a canned announcement that his call was important and might be monitored for better service, he visualized the grand house, a museum really, where pre-Colombian bowls stood side by side with ancient Chinese vases under the watchful eyes of oil portraits of kings and generals, where priceless folios and books and stamps sat in their atmosphere-regulated rooms, where marble figures glinted in the evening light, where federal desks and early American rockers and Native American artifacts were carefully stored and tagged, where glass, so much glass—cranberry, crystal, Tiffany—crowded on shelves, where priceless Middle Eastern rugs and Chinese rugs and Indian rugs waited for the knife, the hammer, the drill, and the saw, waited for the human being to continue his lesson. And what was the point, after all? Oh, he knew. Mr. Kraft, behold the proof that the human being matters. Here is proof that we stand for something.

So beautiful was this vision that he nearly missed the call. "Oh, I'm sorry," he said. "This is the Reverend Richard Wilcox, and I have a very ill family member in Seattle." He explained the bind he was in. Yes, first class would be fine. Would they accept cash? He would even agree to buy a round-trip ticket, but the problem was that his credit cards were stolen right on the beach at Waikīkī, and he was depending on his church to raise the money—there was so little time.

She was so helpful. Of course. There was room, and he would not have to fly standby. If he got to the airport two hours in advance, he would have his ticket, and she hoped that Mr. Wilcox's sister would be all right. He looked at his watch. He did need to get going, collect what he needed from his apartment. But it was no problem.

"Bless you," he said. "Bless us all."

It was difficult for him to keep from laughing with a kind of insane glee. The walls were nine-inch tongue-and-groove boards, just like their original house. The view right off the front lawn was of Olomana with its three peaks, and beyond that, the Ko'olau Mountains and the Pali. It was pure. It was a two-bedroom one-bath tract house built in 1949, with little change from the original. It even had the iron railing for the concrete front steps twisted in decorative loops, just like the railing of the house he once owned. It was on a seven thousand-square-foot lot. It had new shingles. It had a very old electric stove. It was a post-and-beam house with that cool area of dirt underneath, no more rubble than what appeared to be cat crap.

Once upon a time he lived in a house like this, and would now live in this house. Natalie would be furious, but of course would allow it because it showed gumption rather than complacency. She didn't need him anyway.

As he stood there on the lawn, wondering who his new neighbors might be, especially that house across the street with blue tarps covering cars and sunbleached toys on the parched front lawn, the dealer, Ms. Sakuma, was inside on her phone with the owner presenting his offer of ten thousand dollars above the asking price of $549,000, an astonishing figure considering that he bought his original house for $31,000, in 1973. But recapturing the past cost big bucks. In any case, he had the money, in fact far more. He had spent his adult life seeing to that.

Once upon a time, a man who found an alternate life in his imagination, one richer and more fulfilling than his real life, decided to pursue it. He would live in beautiful solitude, interrupted perhaps by the visitations of friends who would eat food he would cook on a hibachi resting on the close-cropped grass rather than on a five-thousand-dollar stainless steel propane atrocity of the sort he saw these days in virtually every house he visited, or rather, every house his wife dragged him to, where he drank his Scotch and talked with people he did not want to talk to, about subjects that did not interest him. Now he would cut his hedge with a machete. He would organize a block party with beer and teri and rice. He would buy Portuguese sausage and sweet bread from kids raising money for their soccer uniforms. He would blow off cubic yards of illegal fireworks every New Year's Eve. And that beautiful girl would always be at his side.

It would be called his "midlife crisis." His children would be pissed and embarrassed, but mostly for themselves: hey, Dad, who else'll know about this? Oh, Dad, sorry, gotta go. I'll get back to you later. Natalie would do fine. For some years now he had suspected that she was doing far better than he might have imagined, and these suspicions only saddened him. It was too much trouble to confront her about it anyway. Life had been comfortable and good, generally.

Ms. Sakuma bustled out onto the tiny wooden porch and said, "They're not waiting. They said yes."

"Good," he said. "What do we do now?"

"We'll need to start the papers, but the best thing would first be to indicate the commitment with a thousand-dollar advance payment."

"No problem," he said. "I'll go get a bank check." He looked at his watch. "They close in an hour and a half."

"As for the mortgage loan—"

"There will be no mortgage," he said. "I plan to pay cash."

She nodded, staring at him. "I know you from somewhere, but I can't—"

"Nat Duncan is my wife."

"Really?" Her eyes widened. "So this is an investment then?"

"Of sorts."

"I've known Nat for twenty years," she said. "I just didn't make the connection. But she's the tiger."

"Absolutely."

"Interesting that she'd want this as an investment."

"No, I want it as an investment."

"We don't know when all of this will bottom out."

"No. I'm doing this I guess partly for reasons of, well, nostalgia. Now that I think of it, the word 'nostalgia' sounds like an affliction, doesn't it? Neuralgia, aphasia, dementia, and so on?"

She laughed uncertainly.

"But I like this house," he said. "And after all, you can't beat real estate as an investment, right?"

"That's right," she said. "You always win with property."

She went back inside to her phone. He looked down the front lawn to the top of his Lexus. He should trade that in on a, let's see, a two-year-old Rav 4 maybe, to go with his what? His yellow plastic kayak and a wooden picnic table for the front lawn. He would plant two papaya trees to balance the immense mango tree over there, and he supposed that, since he could afford it, he would need a yard person. He would consult with Em about that. In fact he would pay Em handsomely to be his yard person. Or perhaps George.

In the meantime, he had to find a place to stay until he could move in, unless there was some way to do it right away by buying an inflatable mattress. His Lexus was half filled with what he wanted: clothes for work, and the sum total of everything he really wanted to have with him, not much, because when he had gone through the house looking for "his stuff" he found very little that he wanted or needed. Fortunately, modern technology made it so that he could take his business with him. The cell phone he instructed his clients to contact if they wanted him, and the wireless laptop that had all his accounts. He had the ticklish urge to go out and find a good eighties Volkswagen Bug to go with the Rav 4.

It was stupid, the whole thing. Ken up there on Hal's weird ladder made of branches hacking away with the hatchet while Hal stood below with his arms folded, watching. Sure, it had seemed simple enough, but Hal had refused to accept the idea that the thick root, or whatever it was, had all this time been holding the top of that cave up.

Now, as they drove in silence down the highway toward Kailua, she wondered what was on Hal's mind while he sat there in the back seat with his eyes closed and a sour, distant look on his face. Ken was driving, looking from time to time over at her as she sat in the front seat, that silly smile on his face, and the occasional shrug of, well, that's the way it goes I guess.

And George. She realized when they'd arrived at the parking lot that she should have claimed the need to pee and gone into the woods to call him, but it was too late by then, and besides, she hadn't seen him at all, which meant that he might not have been there.

"You can drop me off in front of the intermediate school," she said to Ken. "I'm just half a block in."

"I don't know where that is," Ken said.

"I'll show you when we get there."

She sighed and sat back in the leather seat. Smelled good. She should look into this model.

Stupid, bone-headed, short-sighted, hasty, hell, there were plenty of words for it. There was something about his excitement that had blocked out reason. He'd had this irritated and impatient look on his face, and any time poor Ken suggested anything, he blew it off with this superior tone of voice: you just let me decide how we do this, Ken. Would that be okay with you?

So Ken had started hacking away at the thick root, from time to time looking around at them with that same goofy expression, like, do you want me to go on with this? And it had begun to get hot. They stood there, Hal with his arms folded, waiting. When Ken was halfway through the root, he stopped to wipe his forehead with his hand and then squinted at the root. There was some subtle movement. The bark had begun to bulge a little. "We got a problem here," Ken said.

"Keep at it," Hal said.

Ken began working his way down the ladder. He turned and said, "I'm not too sure about that."

"Keep at it."

Just as Ken started to climb the ladder again, she saw that the root had begun to expand, and was subtly expanding more. Ken stopped, watched. The bark bulged off the side of it and made a sort of half bubble, and then there was a weird sigh from the cave, and while Ken jumped down off the ladder, the sigh produced a faint puff of silt dust, at which there was a soft "krumpf" sound she felt in the ground like a miniature earthquake, a couple of birds flying up, and then they could no longer see any opening, or maybe a small opening on one side that nobody would be able to crawl into. Then there was another subtle rumbling in the ground.

Hal climbed partway up the ladder to look. "What we have here," he said, "is a slight topographical adjustment that, shall we say, closes the door for us."

"Can't we dig?"

"With what?" he asked. "Do you think I can drive a fucking backhoe in here? A Caterpillar?"

"You don't need to use that tone with me, Hal."

"Indeed not," he said, coming down off the ladder and wiping his hands together. "I'll have to think about this."

"Bringing more wood in to support the ceiling would have worked better," she'd said.

And he'd said, "Really." So she'd waved the conversation off and looked at her watch.

Ken now looked around doubtfully. "Straight ahead here," she said. "Go past the fire station and turn right. Just a little beyond that you can drop me off."

"Okay," he said.

It was late afternoon already. She turned to Hal and said, "Listen, give me a call if you have any other questions about the house."

He opened his eyes. "House?"

"Your house."

"Oh yes," he said, and sat up and rubbed his eyes. "Speaking of which, I'm going to go home, shower, and relax. Been a long day." He looked at her, an apologetic expression on his face. "Listen, sorry about that back at the cave," he said. "But you know, nothing ventured, nothing gained." He winked.

She flushed a little. "Well, you're right." She saw the school on the right. "You can drop me here," she said to Ken.

"You know," Hal said, "the one thing that I thought of while we were leaving is that we didn't see anything in the cave, right?"

"Right."

"There were gouges in the silt inside."

"That's what they said."

"Which means we may not have been at the right cave anyway." He held his hand up, a pained expression on his face. "This is not the sour grapes thing, okay? It was no more than a good try, and I guess we have to accept that."

"I accept it," she said.

She got out at the beginning of her street. When they drove off, she stood there, then looked at her watch. Hm. Had to check the calendar, because as she recalled, they were supposed to go to Kāhala tonight to visit the Masons, who had a nice place but not on the beach. She began walking home, and snorted. All that money they had, and they picked a place a block off the beach. It baffled her.

Then she remembered poor George the Hulk. She pulled out her cell phone and dialed him up.

"Yes?"

"We're done, George," she said. "Are you still up there? Did you ever get up there? I didn't see your car."

"I'm up here, and you told me to park it someplace away from the lot, so I parked down at the bottom in that little road by the traffic light and walked up. But those men didn't see it."

"Didn't see what?"

"When the thing fell. It opened up on top. I'm looking at it now. I can see inside."

"What do you see, George?"

"Dirt."

She told him to wait by the trail and so he waited and it rained. Under a tree he kept the water off his glasses. Every building was perfect. Every cloud in the distance was perfect, rounded and dark on the bottoms. At his feet water trickled, the reflection from the sun making diamonds, the secret sounds of leaves and dirt swelling with the water coming to him in a hushed whisper. He found the skeleton of a leaf, held it up to look through it, the webbing perfect, the symmetry of the tiny squares and triangles so perfect that he held his breath looking at it.

Those men didn't see it. They didn't need glasses but they didn't see it, and he laughed. When that hillside dropped and the dust puffed out, they didn't see the webbed fern at the top of it stretch and rise, like skin, stretching, and after they left he went and looked, placed his foot on the webbing of fern and his foot went through, so he pulled some of it apart and looked and saw the angled gap of an opening that went down into the darkness. You'd think a smart person would see it. The seesawing motion of one door closing while another opened. A bird flew past, dark brown but with white on it, a long tail. A—What was that? A shama thrush. Now he heard it sing in trees below, its melody like a question.

His sneakers were wet. The rain had let up, and he moved out from under the tree and into the sun, remained there above the opening and in view of the trail so he could see her when she came. Stay, she said. You stay right there and I'll be right back. Don't move, George. I'll buy you a house, George.

The proper axis. That was what the eye doctor called it, and when he slid those glasses on his face, the plastic arms sliding over his temples and resting on his ears, he was shocked looking at a white jacket with tan buttons in a line, next to a pocket with three pens in it. He wanted to scream at the rich, watery lucidity of it.

He saw her. She was shaking water from her hair, walking on the trail, a hoe in one hand and a canvas shopping bag in the other. She stopped, put the bag down, and fiddled with something. The phone rang. He pulled it from his pocket and opened it.

"Where are you?"

"Just ahead and below you. See? I'm waving."

A minute later, she stood above on the trail looking down at him. "How do I get there?" she called.

"Go another fifty feet," he said, pointing. "It's not as steep there."

He waited. Then he heard her, waited, and saw her. Her clothes were wet and she looked gleeful and flustered, like someone getting ready to whip someone and enjoy doing it. She was breathless.

"George," she said, and then breathed deliberately. "George, you're my friend, right?"

"Yes ma'am."

"I'll give you plenty if this works out. Plenty."

"Yes ma'am."

"Have you told anyone about this?"

"No, ma'am."

"Can I trust you to help me with this without—" She looked past his feet at the fern. "Without worrying about getting taken advantage of here?"

"Yes."

She looked at the fern. "So what hole were you talking about?"

He made his way farther down the bank to the ferns, stooped down and pulled at them, revealing the gap. She put the hoe and the bag on the wet grass and stood over it.

"Oh," she said. "My god." A foot and a half wide, at maybe a forty-five degree angle, going down into blackness. She reached into her shopping bag and drew out a flashlight, aimed it in. "Oh my god," she said. You could see right down, no more than twelve feet, to where a bed of dark dirt was, appearing dry and flat.

"They didn't see it," he said.

She looked at him, wide-eyed, thinking. "No, they didn't see it. They think this is over. It's just you and me." She laughed then, loud, and looked out toward the ocean. "You and me, George."

"Yes ma'am."

"You can carry lots, can't you George?"

"I can carry a lot, yes."

"I want to make sure this is safe. Do you think it's safe?"

"No."

"Why, George? Why isn't it safe?"

Why did she talk that way? He shrugged, and moved to his right and leaned down to pull at the ferns, which he had pushed back into place after he looked at it the first time. "It's probably all right," he said, pointing. She looked. The three-foot-thick shelf of rock leaned against rock above it, and the shelf got thicker the farther away from that edge it went. "If it doesn't slide, then it's all right," he said.

"That's not sliding," she said. "Even if it did it would stop because the whole roof of this thing isn't going to slide."

Little threads of water ran down the rock face. "Well," he said, "there's a thing that says water is a—a—"

"A what, George? What thing says that?"

"It's just a thing. I can't remember the word. Water makes things slide. Like, a lubricant, that's it."

"All right," she said flatly. "All right. Lubricant I understand. But this isn't moving."

She seemed agitated now. She looked into the gap, sighed quickly, and made her way to the other end of it, and pulled at the ferns. He went to watch. Water trickled down the face of the rock on that side too, right over the place where the corner of the slab met it.

"This water is going to go down into the silt," she said.

"It's still raining up there above us. So more water is coming down, I think."

"Well we can't let it do that." She stood up and folded her arms. "You can't get this close and lose out."

She went to her shopping bag and drew out a coil of rope. She undid it, then fumbled with one end to create a loop. He turned and looked again at the glistening wall of rock, at the corner of the rock leaning against it. Ants walked over part of that rock, over a piece of brown leaf plastered by water to the glittering surface.

"You're going to let me down there holding onto the rope," she said. "I'll put my foot in it like a stirrup, and then you'll hand the hoe down to me, all right?"

"Yes ma'am."

"We're talking here maybe ten to twenty million, George," she said, pointing a finger at him. "When I call, you'll pull me up, right?"

"Yes I will," he said.

"Those assholes probably wouldn't, you know. That's why I asked you to come. I can't trust them. But I can really, really trust you, can't I?"

"Yes." He looked at the rock face. "But the water," he said.

"Let me worry about the water, George." She looked into the hole. "Any box he put in here would be put at the back of it, I suspect. That's where I'll dig first."

She studied the rope, took a deep breath. She looked at him, thinking, and handed him the coil, leaving about five feet of the rope. Then she sat at the edge of the opening and put the little noose around her right sneaker. With her other shoe, experimentally, she kicked the thick edge of the suspended roof of the cave.

"Hah," she said, "steady as a rock."

She was not heavy. He held the rope, let it slide through his hands as she made her way down. Soon she was at the bottom, the upper part of her body between the two rock faces. She slid sideways, drawing the flashlight from her pocket, and stooped over. "I see where someone dug something," she called, a hollow and muffled sound in her voice. "And I see a little light over there." Then she squirmed sideways and he could see her head again. She was standing up again. "George, can you reach down and hand me that hoe? And then pull me up in a few minutes. We have to figure out how to get stuff out. Under my feet I feel stuff, not far under the surface."

"Yes ma'am," he said.

He turned, the rope in one hand, and picked up the hoe, and turned back, holding it by its blade. He got to his knees and then leaned into the hole, his scalp prickling because he did not like having his arm in there, and reached down with it as far as he could.

"Got it," she said. "Put a rock or something on the rope and get the bag; there's another section of rope in there you can hitch it to."

He turned.

"George? Did you hear me?"

"Yes," he said. The ground shocked his heels and he turned and fell in a grinding sound, the glasses slipping down his face so that the sky was full of smoky moving blotches, and he put the glasses on and saw birds wheeling above him.

His heart pounded, and he couldn't breathe. The hole was gone. The cave roof had fallen on it. He reached out to touch the rock, but his hands shook badly. He tried to breathe. The birds settled again into the trees.

"Ma'am," he said. He reached out and pulled at the rope; it came out of the crack flattened and ground off at the end.

She was in there. He pulled the cell phone from his pocket, but his hands would not work. He studied the grid of buttons, then pressed the bottom key in the big square, and the number came up. He held his breath and pushed it.

He could not tell where it came from *da da da de daa.* Faint, as if from the sky or from his memory. *Da da da de daa.* Nothing. A haunting, distant jingle from a bad dream. *Da da da de daa.*

He shut the phone. He breathed, his hand on his chest. Then he got up. Light from the other side. He made his way around the top edge of the crack and then down below to where they had built their ladder, not strong enough to hold him. His legs shook. He reached up to grab a lip of rock, then pulled himself up, got a hand at a little space, and pulled again until his face was near the opening. Wafting from it was a familiar odor, the rich, metallic smell of burst viscera and blood and waste. He knew it. He knew this smell. It was the smell of a slaughterhouse.

He walked away from there. Numb, he knew only that he was walking, sometimes stumbling on roots that crossed the trail. "I am not responsible," he whispered. I am not.

Ahead he heard someone. He climbed up the bank and into the brush, and waited, and a man jogged by with his dog. He went back to the trail. "I am not responsible," he said. "No, not this time. I am not."

He walked. Then he was walking down a slope into near darkness, one patch of light there fifty feet ahead, the leaves and stones and bushes in that patch brilliant in their color. When he got to it, he saw something on the ground, and picked it up. It was half a bird's egg, broken cleanly around the middle. Holding it up into the sunlight on the tip of his little finger, he studied the tiny brownish burgundy dots all over it, against an off-white background, as if someone had shaken a paintbrush at it, the shell resembling a perfect, elliptical thimble.

Billy had picked Derek up at four and they were on their way to the golf course to talk to their former boss.

"Nevah work," Derek said. "'Memba, you tol' him he could put the whole golf course up his ass."

"Did I really say that?"

"Yeah. But you know him, and you 'memba what he say."

"I don't," Billy said.

"He say, 'what, which end you wan' me to start wit'?' You laughed, too."

"Oh yeah, now I recall."

Derek stared at him. "Recall?"

"Sorry brah. Now I 'memba. It's dis language shit my, ah, former boss wen' push on me. I had to practice talkin' like one haole."

"You'll get ovah dat."

"Like I tol' you, I wen' punch him ah? Was one disagreement thing like I said. I tol' him come out hea take us on, wit' alla mainlan' bangers he can call up. So right now I keeping watch on my ass, if you catch my drif'."

"Shit, we sen' um home callin' dea dentisses and doctahs ah? You need any, I call frien's. Stick wit' us, you be okay."

They pulled along to the gate, where Ricky Nagasako stepped out, looked, and then laughed. "Eh, what? Slumming?"

"No, I just thought I'd go try to get my job back," Billy said. "Derek too."

"'Kay," and he waved them on.

Marty Ching was a beefy, easy-going guy who constantly ragged on his clueless employees, and he wanted to run a classy operation. You have to know how to relate to rich people, how to carry their bags, polish off their clubs at the end of the day. You get right to them and you pick up their bags. You call them "sir" and you keep yourself clean, no dirty fingernails, your hair combed, no flashy court shoes or shorts whose crotches hang below the knees. No iPods. When they talk, act interested, no matter what they're saying.

Billy felt a little nervous doing this, having to eat crow or, he supposed, eat shit, to try to get his job back. He pulled into the parking lot, and he and Derek got out. Derek, shit, he'd get his job back garans, because Marty liked him. Billy on the other hand would have to, what? Grovel? He wouldn't do that. He would simply ask for the job back and if Marty said no, then he'd get in his car and bag.

Marty saw them just as he was grinding a cigarette out on the blacktop and picking the butt up to throw it in a rubbish can. He squinted, saw Billy, and got that look, that what the fuck are you doing here? look, and Billy waved, shaka-ed him just for good measure. They walked toward him, Billy looking around and thinking that after all, this course was really beautiful, and something struck him while they were walking: just beyond Marty was the mountain range, the Koʻolaus, and low on those flanks was the trail. His heart did a strange flop in his chest, because of what he had decided he could not do, and he was tempted to hate himself for that, but shook it off. If the stuff belonged to that dork's family then it was up to that dork to find it, not Billy. Besides, Derek was his friend, and if the dork and Terry were hooking up, that was their business and he couldn't do anything about it. He would not hate himself. There were some things people didn't understand, Pinchot particularly, and he had to stick to his guns. But the recollection of punching Pinchot, and all the shit that he had said to him, gave him a feeling of achievement, why, he didn't know.

"Gentlemen," Marty Ching said. "What, you like play golf?"

"Nah nah nah," Derek said. "We like owa o' jobs back."

"Billy," Marty said. "Really? What about your other job? The one that was going to make you so much money?"

"I like this job," he said. "It was my mistake. That other job isn't the kind that's appropriate for me, I think. So I'd appreciate the chance to work here again."

Marty Ching stared at him, a long time. He pulled out a cigarette and lit it, put his lighter back in his pocket. "Where you went? College?"

"Excuse me?"

"The way you talk. What happened?"

Billy felt a sudden embarrassment. "Oh," he said. "I can talk any way you want, I guess. I just want my job back."

"So," Marty said, puffing on his cigarette, "what was your hourly?"

"Eleven fifty."

"You gotta start lower this time. Is that okay? We can waive the application."

"That would be suitable," Billy said.

Derek stared at him.

"I mean," Billy said. "That would be cool."

"So we plant them tomorrow?"

"Yeah, best to get them out of the pots and in the ground as soon as you can," Em said. She pictured them, three trees in black plastic pots, sitting under the eave of Mrs. Ikeda's house. They had spent a good deal of time selecting them, and then figuring out how to fit them into the back of the car without spilling cinder all over the place. One ended up on the front floor, some of the branches coming up between her legs. Because Mrs. Ikeda was not home, they put them against the side of the house, and left. Now she pictured the stuff in the trunk, their backpacks, the wooden statue with the two shell eyes. And she shuddered a little.

"Uh," Em said. Then he turned back to the traffic. He thought for a few seconds, and then turned his head slightly. "Uh, you said 'we' in reference to planting the trees. Does that mean you want to come by tomorrow, I mean to Mrs. Ikeda's?"

"Oh, sure," she said. "I can help. It depends on who's manning the phones and stuff, but I can help after work."

"Okay. But I was thinking, like, this whole thing might be over. I mean, unless we still do that stuff with the digger and all that. If it's okay, I'd appreciate the help I guess."

"I'll help."

She sat there watching the blue hood of the car sweeping over the blacktop. So it was over. He was right.

He continued driving, and he was still thinking. "Should I drop you off at your house now?"

"Could I come to your house first?" Actually she didn't want to go her house. Only to *yes* pour it out, she thought.

"Sure."

So he drove along. The tools rattled in the back seat. She knew why she didn't want to go home now. She wanted to continue to work on the project in the apartment, because she didn't like unfinished cleaning projects. She didn't like unfinished anything and something wasn't finished and it bothered her. It wasn't the cleaning project. That would be finished. Something else was not anywhere near being finished. She didn't know what it was, only that it was, and whatever it was was wrong. She fingered the bone hook hanging on her chest. She would have to give it back.

"If it's okay," Em said, "I'd like to show that statue to Millie Leong. She knows about that kind of stuff."

"Oh, yeah, you should," she said.

He drove, down past the hospital toward his apartment. That was one of the unfinished things: Mrs. Leong. "Can we stop at Longs and buy a fan for her?" she asked.

"Hey, that's a good idea," he said. "We'll do that. Actually they have good ones at the hardware store."

They went to the hardware store instead of Longs, which was near his apartment. They bought a little Vornado that had three speeds, and put the box on top of the tools in the back seat.

He pulled around into his street. There was a space waiting for him. "Wow," he said. "That's folca for you."

Inside the apartment, they put their backpacks down on the couch and Em opened the back sliding door to let air through. The fan was in its box on the floor. The remaining work on the living room was there, and she stared at the bags, envelopes, and other junk. Once that was done, what else would there be? She didn't know *nothing maybe* and she waited while Em watered the orchids outside.

All through buying the trees and taking them to Mrs. Ikeda's, he hadn't mentioned anything else about the cave, except when they were driving back. That relieved her in a way, because she didn't think she wanted to get near that opening again. She might go in. Horrible as it would be, she didn't trust herself not to try it. It was true, though, that he mentioned some tool they could make to dig from the outside, so maybe there was more to this, some extension of the project. Maybe next week or something. But that wasn't it.

Em's backpack was lying on the couch and the two shell eyes were looking at her. She reached down and slid the wooden image out of the case and held it up. It felt warm. The eyes looked at her, the simplified carved face with its full lips and lump of a nose, and the body of the statue, with its half-closed legs and pointed breasts, looked full and dense and somehow alive. It was like there was soft chatter around its head. Then she felt a weird swoon, a sensation of emptying, so that a warm shudder made its way through her flesh, and she held her breath, staring at the two shell eyes, and felt the urge to cry. She fought it off, staring at the eyes, looking once through the kitchen at a glittering fan of water sweeping across the bright opening. She put the image down on the couch, and stood there. She felt light. She felt as if she had lost weight standing there, and didn't know why, and it scared her.

Em came in, stopped, and stared at her. "You okay?" he asked.

"I—Yeah, I think so."

"Do you want to take the fan to Mrs. Leong? And show her the statue?"

"Uh, yeah, let's take it. Let's do that."

It was like nothing she'd felt before—she was floating down past those doors in a dream, light and weird and airy and breathless. She was aware that Em was taking the fan from the box amid all sorts of mahalos and oh my's and Em that's so nice, and once it had started, lightly riffling the hem of Mrs. Leong's dress, Em turned and picked up the image and held it out to her, and she took it as if it were a baby, staring at it, her mouth slightly open.

"Em, dis one fertility goddess," she said.

"Really?"

Then she didn't hear what else they were saying because she was staring at the wooden image, holding her breath.

Within a minute they were walking back, Em holding the image out before him and Terry floating behind him staring at her feet trying to figure out why she felt no pressure up from the ground when she placed them there, and once inside the apartment, she stood in the middle of the living room trying to figure it out, and Em stepped in front of her, and stared.

"Are you all right?"

"I'm fine. I—"

"I said what should we do about maybe getting something to eat?"

She looked at him. What was it? She looked at her feet, holding her breath. There was an airiness. A space. She thought she should be frightened but she wasn't.

"She went away," she whispered.

"Who?"

"She—Oh, I'm sorry, I was just thinking of—"

She went away. The chatter was somewhere else, nearby but somewhere else. She could almost hear it, girlish chatter somewhere else.

"So we can go eat?" he asked, moving toward the door.

"No." She stepped between him and the door. "I mean, we can eat here. I can cook something."

"I don't have anything."

"Can I look?" Em didn't seem to understand. "I mean in your kitchen?"

"Uh, sure," he said.

She floated toward the kitchen and understood it there. That was why she wanted to eat here and not somewhere else. Company. Chatter. She opened the refrigerator. He was right. There was half a jar of medium garlic salsa, a little bit of cheese, some milk, and a couple of cans of Bud Light.

She opened a cupboard. Canned beans. A box of macaroni. She stared at the macaroni, remembered the garlic salsa, the cheese. "I got it," she said. She took a pot from the counter, checked to make sure it was clean, filled it half full with water, and put the burner on high.

"Uh, maybe—"

"No, you'll see."

There were two cans of Vienna sausages in the cupboard. Ordinarily she would not eat Vienna sausages, but she opened them both. These she would mix with the salsa and cheese, and stir in with the cooked macaroni. It would work.

About the Author

A resident of Hawaiʻi since 1966, the late Ian MacMillan authored seven novels and five short story collections, one of which won the Associated Writing Programs Award for Short Fiction, before his passing in 2008. He made over a hundred appearances in literary and commercial magazines including *Yankee, The Sun, Paris Review, Iowa Review,* etc., and his work was reprinted in *Best American Short Stories, Pushcart Prize,* and *O. Henry Award* volumes, among other "best" anthologies. Winner of the 1992 Hawaiʻi Award for Literature, he taught fiction writing at the University of Hawaiʻi. His novels include *The Red Wind* and *The Braid* from Mutual Publishing (1998), and *Village of a Million Spirits: A Novel of the Treblinka Uprising* from Steerforth Press and Penguin Books (2000), which won the 2000 PEN U.S.A.-West Fiction Award.